THROUGH THIN WALLS

Gail Proctor

Contents

16. Epilogue

Chapter 1

Someone was playing music as if they had a party going at 9.45 in the morning. Of course that was a possibility. The chances that someone was hosting a 'morning-after' party the morning after New Years were pretty reasonable.

I carried myself up the staircase, already looking forward to getting settled. I hated unpacking, even if I didn't own much. It was dull and counterproductive. Especially when you hardly were home.

I reached the third floor and found the right door. 34B. That was me.

And apparently the party-music was my neighbors. Lovely.

I threw my box down on the floor in front of my door and started searching through my pockets for my key. The one I literally just picked up from the landlord two floors down. It would be a new record if I already managed to lose it.

And you're a detective. You find things for a living, my sarcastic inner voice reminded me.

"For fuck's sake," I cursed under my breath, finally finding the damn key. Just as I was putting the key into the keyhole, my neighbors door swung open with a wham.

"... don't fucking understand you, Amy, you're a piece of work, you know that?!" Some guy who was pulling on his jacket shouted into the apartment. He was obviously pissed, purely judging from his words, to the sound of his angry voice and the sneer on his face. His short black hair was tousled and his clothes looked wrinkled—never mind the stench of alcohol hanging around him like the worst cologne in the world.

"Nobody forced you to come by last night Maddox, if you want to blame someone for making stupid decisions, blame yourself." A female voice suddenly spoke. While the guy was heading towards the staircase, my eyes drifted to the woman who appeared in the doorway, wearing nothing but an oversized man's shirt and dear God, I hoped underwear. Her makeup was smeared under her eyes and her brown hair that clearly had been curled with a curling iron last night was messy and thrown into a careless bun on top of her head. She held a cigarette in between her fingers, and as soon as she saw me there, her eyes did a take of me, just like I did her.

"Who are you?" She questioned while the Maddox-guy stomped down the stairs with muffled angry curses.

I lifted the key in my hand. "Your new neighbor."

"Oh," She said, her eyebrows shooting upwards, obviously caught by surprise. "Well I guess you just got your warm welcome to the building then. Sorry about that," She glanced after Maddox. "I'm Amy."

"Russell," I replied, trying to keep my eyes peeled on her face. Yeah, even if she had all the signs of the 'morning-after-having-just-fucked' look, she was admittedly hot. Long legs I could tell were exercised from dancing, cute toes that probably curled a lot last night, elegant fingers which were probably skilled in the art of clawing, a sculpted décolletage that accentuated her slender neck—

You're deducing. Stop.

"Nice to meet you," She held out her hand—after popping the cigarette in between her plump lips—and I gave it a shake. As suspected, she had soft hands.

"Likewise."

"I'll let you return to moving in," She said, blowing out a cloud of smoke, the smell like torture to my nearly-five-months-nicotine-free body. "Feel free to knock on my door if you need something. Anything."

I studied her face, counting the possibilities of that having a doubling meaning. She wasn't a prostitute, that much I could tell, but she was offering me, after having just kicked a guy out who clearly rang the new year in between her legs.

"Right, thanks," I replied, gritting my teeth. "I'll keep that sound in mind."

With a smile that could only be described as seductive, Amy took a step backwards into her still-booming-with-music apartment and closed the door.

"I'm certainly not in Kansas anymore," I said to myself, before unlocking my own door. Picking up my box, I walked in.

Plain white walls. Light wooden floors. Bed and bathroom in one end; living room and kitchen in the other. The apartment was already slightly furnished with an old couch, a bed and a nightstand, but that was about it. This was my new home.

I dumped the box down on the floor again and ran my hand through my hair, sighing heavily. This was so different from Wichita. The vibe was different, the sun was brighter here. Of course Miami Florida was known as the sunshine state, so that pretty much spoke for itself. Still, even knowing that, it was still such a big change from my humdrum life back in Kansas. Yet not one part of me missed it.

After about two minutes of contemplating just ditching the rest of my shit down in my car, I convinced myself to go get it. All the while the music next door kept booming. Three trips up and down the stairs later, my six pathetic boxes of crap stood in my apartment, already cluttering.

Just then, saving me from the idea of actually unpacking, my phone rang. I pulled it out of my pocket and flipped it open. "Crane."

"We got a case for you, Detective. They're asking specifically for you."

Closing my eyes and leaning my head back, I felt a smile slide on to my lips. "20 minutes, I'm coming in."

After nine hours of talking to the police, visiting the scene of the crime which was a real fucking mess I might add, then going back to the police station to go through the evidence, then questioning the witnesses myself, and then finally, having been handed over all the files I needed, I was back in my apartment which was as empty and lonely as I left it. My boxes had already collected the first specs of dust, but I couldn't be bothered. I was lying on top of my bed, going through the files with a bottle of gin in my hand.

Yeah, you're the best fucking detective out there, my inner sarcastic voice drawled. Drinking while working. Classy. Where's that medal they gave you?

Working a muscle in my jaw, I flipped a page and scanned the evidence. Even if I fucking got wasted to the point of drooling while speaking, I could still solve a case in less than a week and that was when I was drunk. When I wasn't, cases like these could be solved in days. At best, hours. That's why the police contacted me. Because I was the best there was.

"Oh, yes..."

I was pretty sure that wasn't my inner voice giving me a pat on the back. Even in my half-drunken state of inebriation, I knew for certain that that didn't come from my head.

"Ahh, fuck yes!"

I turned and glared back at my wall, the one my headboard was faced up against. As if it was the wall that had spoken, I frowned at it. What the hell?

"Oh God, yes, yes, yes, ahh, fuck!"

What. The actual. Fuck.

My wall was thinner than a goddamn sheet of paper. I recognized the voice as my neighbor's; Amy. And based on the sounds she was making, it would seem that her and that Maddox-guy, had made up after their argument.

I scoffed. Wonderful. I got to hear them fuck all night now.

When the sounds continued and my concentration faltered, I balled up my fist and was prepared to knock on the wall to let them know they were being loud. But then my hand froze as I heard her next words—her next moan.

"Oh, Russell!"

CHAPTER 2

I closed my folder, listening as my neighbor climaxed while panting my name.

Well, this was new one.

Alright, options; One, she happened to have a second lover whose name also happened to be Russell. Chances? Bleak. First off, I didn't believe in coincidences, and second of all, I couldn't hear any male company.

Two; ... there was none. My neighbor was masturbating to the memory of meeting me.

... I literally had no idea how to react.

Her soft moans finally dialed down as her orgasm subsided, leaving me with complete silence. My conclusion was that she had gone to sleep.

Opening my folder again, I tried to zone back into work-mode, but my brain wouldn't let me. There was a big possibility that Amy, my neighbor, was one kinky woman.

The only question left in my head then was... did she know I could hear her?

I plugged in my coffee-maker, just as my cellphone rang. I answered. "This better be about the case."

"It is, Mr Crane. How far are you?"

Letting out a breath, I rubbed my face. "I didn't get much work done last night."

"Mr Crane, you know we rely on you to be fast and efficient. Your social events or other activities will have to be set aside when a murderer is on the loose, so from now on—"

"Ms Dee, with all do respect, I put my every minute and second into my job and you know that. When I say I didn't get much work done last night, it's not because I was being lazy or had company, but if you're unhappy with my performance, go ahead and fire me. Let's see how fast your newbies will solve this one."

When I heard nothing in the other end, I knew I had won. Ms Erika Dee was my 'boss' or employer, if you would. I didn't have a signed contract with the Miami police and didn't plan on getting one, but whenever they were stumped on a mystery case, they came to me. We both knew that if she fired me right now, the murder case she had given me would take weeks to get solved.

"Fine," She finally snapped. "But you're on thin ice, Crane."

"That's where I like to be."

She huffed in annoyance through the phone. "I expect to see you here at the station in forty-five minutes. Are we clear?"

I smirked, getting my one mug out of my moving box. "As ice."

I frustratedly ran my hands through my hair for what seemed like the millionth time. Incompetent fools could make you go bald like this.

"I'm going to explain it one last time," I growled, glaring at Ms Dee and the client. "Your husband faked the robbery, had the deeds to your summer house stolen on purpose, then sold it to an investor, only to buy it back after the divorce, so when the papers finally got signed, you wouldn't get it. Your husband cheated on you and he therefore knew the court would favor you. He'd wind up broke and divorced, but at least this way, he'd have his summer house." I said for what also seemed like the millionth time. "Hats off to your husband for being clever. Everything you'll need to sue him is in this folder," I said, pointing to a manila folder on the conference table where we were sitting. "The evidence, the money wires, even pictures of him enjoying himself in Costa Rica with a Brazilian woman. Knock yourself out."

Ms Cortez, recently divorced with her botoxed lips and drawn-on eyebrows extended a long manicured finger and pointed to the folder. "You got all that from just reading a file?"

I leaned back in the leather coated chair and tiredly closed my eyes. "It was obvious if someone cared to actually investigate."

"But how?" Ms Cortez drawled in a Brazilian accent. "You have never met my husband, how could you know what he would do?"

"Have you met your husband?" I countered. "Oh, but I get it. You were too blinded with love to notice what kind of man he was. Money and a private jet can do that to you."

"Mr Crane!" Ms Dee snapped, sending me a lethal glare. "That's enough! Ms Cortez, I am terribly sorry—"

"Let me finish, Ms Cortez asked herself," I interrupted, sitting up in my chair again. I met Ms Cortez' shocked eyes. "From his photo alone, you can tell he's a man who enjoys being powerful. He has the same taste in friends as he has in women," I eyed her up and down, taking in her surgically enhanced breasts and orange tan, "Fake and usually money grabbers—"

"Mr Crane!"

"—so naturally when I ran a background check on him, I wasn't surprised to find him being involved with loan sharks, rich investors, bankers, and a few other criminal business-es. After that, all I had to do was put myself in his shoes; I'm cheating on my Brazilian wife with another Brazilian woman—obviously I have a distinct taste—and my house is in Costa Rica, Brazil. If you were about to get divorced, wouldn't you make sure you could escape to a bachelor pad in a country where you're surrounded by what you love?" I pause, taking a moment to enjoy Ms Cortez hanging jaw. "The rest was really just elementary."

Ms Cortez looked absolutely flabbergasted and lost for words. Eventually it ended up with Ms Dee throwing me out of the room while she stayed behind to console the horrified Ms Cortez. Finally, after thirty minutes or so, Ms Dee exited the conference room with a scowl on her face. She aimed straight towards me.

"Mr Crane," She started, her voice dripping with venom. She pushed her thin glasses up on her nose, giving me a lethal glare. "Out of all the unforgivable, foolish, tasteless things you've ever done while working for us—"

"I don't work for you, I work with you," I interrupted and crossed my arms. "You came to me with this case. Ms Cortez wanted me to personally solve it and I did. Whatever follows is a product of her own misplaced questions; She asked about my methods and I replied. I can't be bothered if she doesn't like the truth. And as for you," I snapped, sending her a glare that matched her own. "You know that these kind of tedious cases are beneath me and I never bore myself with them. Next time you throw a client at me like that in the flash of the moment, I will quit all by myself. I chose which cases I want; not the client. Now, if you'll excuse me."

I left the station, feeling Ms Dee's stunned persona glaring after me.

Returning to the bloody case I had been trying to read last night, I now gave it another attempt. Sitting on my living room couch this time, I was certain I wouldn't be disturbed here. Unfortunately, that wasn't the case.

Three short knocks sounded on my door and my mind immediately deduced it to be a woman's knuckles meeting my wooden door. They were light, yet firm.

Sighing, I threw the file down on the couch before standing up and walking to my door. I couldn't say I was surprised when I opened it and found Amy standing there.

"Hi," She smiled at me, putting a hand on the doorframe. "Did I wake you?"

Was it late? I had no idea. Time was useless unless some crazy killer gave you a timeline. "No. What can I do for you?"

My eyes scanned her body and I couldn't help but notice she looked a lot more decent than the first time we met. Of course she wasn't curing a bad hangover with sex now and her New Year's makeup and hair wasn't discriminating her natural beauty anymore. Her brown locks were naturally wavy and her eyes were brown with dark lashes. Her lips were cream colored and the skin around her clavicle bone was sunkissed. You could faintly see a bikini tan-line where her flimsy nightgown wasn't covering her. We were in Miami; her going to the beach wasn't surprising.

"Do you have any batteries?"

That, on the other hand, was.

It took a lot to actually catch me off guard, but she had succeeded marvelously. Her question, as innocent and benign as it was, was to me anything but that. Judging on what I had been an intrigued listener to last night, I'd say her battery operated device had lost its juice.

"Batteries." I repeated. It wasn't a question, more like a statement, if you could even call batteries that. In this case it was. "How many do you need?"

"Just two."

"Let me guess; A+?"

She blinked, a little surprised. "Yes? How did you know?"

Without replying, I went to my boxes that still waited to be unpacked and rummaged through them for my old flashlight.

In the meantime Amy stepped inside my apartment, giving it a curious glance.

"Your place looks a bit empty," She noted, sauntering into my living room. She ran her hand across my couch.

Pausing for a moment to glance after her comfortable intrusion of my home, I slowly trailed my eyes up her legs to her rear. "I don't find much need for material supplies in my life."

"Really?" She said, noticing the case folder. She picked it up, looking at the bold CONFIDENTIAL letters. "And what exactly is it that you do with your life that requires so little?"

I grabbed the batteries from my flashlight and walked up to her. Her eyes shifted to me as I stopped in front of her, closer than what was needed. I looked down at her. "I'm a detective."

I saw her pupils expand and then she slowly licked her lip. "A detective, hm? Are you any good?"

Glancing down at her mouth, I replied. "The best."

A smirk quirked to her lip and she rose a questionable brow. "A little cocky, don't you think?"

"It's the truth." I replied. "Would you like me to make a deduction?"

Her smirk only grew. "By all means."

"You're a sex addict," I said, taking a step back from her to observe her body. Her smirk immediately froze. "I noticed your legs were trained when we met yesterday and I assumed it was from dancing, but it's not, is it?" I rhetorically questioned. "It's exercise from the morbidly big amount of sex you have, and clearly, your appetite is hardly ever sated.

Based on the words I caught from that guy Maddox, he's an ex-boyfriend whom on several occasions has been your booty-call whenever life got so depressing you needed a distraction from your sad existence. Obviously there's some tension left between you two, hence his crude words to you, not to mention your reply, which, if I may add, I found truly fascinating." I smiled satisfied when her face paled and her breath started to quicken. "I also further deduce that you're a nymphomaniac."

"W-what?" She breathed, taken aback. "A n-nymphoma—"

"A nymphomaniac. Someone who lives off of collecting trophies in the shape of men." I stepped closer to her, invading her personal space again. "I bet you keep a picture of each man you've ever dated or slept with."

Amy blinked up at me, partial shock and partial offense painting her face. I was hitting her spot-on. "And on what grounds do you make that deduction?" She swallowed.

I took the final step between us and took her hand. She looked down as I opened her palm and placed the two A+ batteries inside it. "Next time you moan my name while masturbating, don't expect me to act ignorant. Just like you came here tonight acting all innocent like you didn't plan on scoring me. I know."

We were a hair's width apart. Amy looked up at me stunned, confused, but never humiliated. She exhaled shakily before breathing the one word everyone asked me; "How?"

I pursed my lips a little. "I could start a long deduction to explain why, but since it's late and you're obviously impatient to go back to your apartment to masturbate, I'll keep it simple;" I surprised her by pressing a knee in between her legs, grazing her sex. She gasped. "You're wet."

CHAPTER 3

"**D**on't look so surprised," I said, watching as her lips parted and turned into an 'o' shape. "You came here with an agenda and I'm a detective. It's my job to know."

Slowly, she closed her mouth and inhaled deeply. "You really are good."

"I never exaggerate, I find that despite popular belief, it doesn't promote understanding but rather falsifies the information." I took a step back from her, walking over to my kitchen.

"Do you always talk like that?"

"Like what?"

"Like you fucked Merriam Webster." I heard Amy's footsteps follow me to my coffeemaker. She put the batteries I gave her down on the counter. "Is that just how you speak or is it to impress me?"

"Why would I want to impress you?" I questioned while taking the coffee pot and putting it under the tap to fill it. "You clearly already find me attractive if we go by your soaked undergarments."

"No arguments there," She chided. "Normally I don't go for blond men, but those curls are irresistible. I like hair that's long enough to drag my fingers through in throes of an ōrgasm. Pardon my language."

"Is that what you pictured when you were touching yourself last night?"

"Of course."

There was a moment of silence that was only broken by the coffeemaker brewing. She was giving me all the clearest invitations to join the party between her legs, save for maybe holding up a banner that said 'fuck-me.' She was upfront and I liked that. But was it enough?

"I don't do relationships," I curtly said when I felt her staring at me from the side. "My work is always my first priority."

"I don't do relationships either," Amy replied. I heard her take a few steps towards me, until I felt her hand land on my shoulder blade. "I'm all about the sex."

Her hand slid down the broadness of my back to the start of my pants. The other tickled my neck.

I swiftly turned around, caught her in my arms and locked her against me. She faintly gasped from the surprise and placed her palms on my pecs. "Alright, Amy. You have my attention. Use it well."

She met my eyes. Her chestnut brown pupils dilated until they turned almost onyx. She slowly brought her hand to the front of my hair, gripping it. Teasing my curls between her fingers, she pulled my head down to her face. I came closer, stopping when we were but a hair's width apart. She frowned annoyed. "What?"

I studied her face for what was probably two seconds, but felt like minutes.

There was something... about her. Something I couldn't yet put my finger on and it annoyed me. I didn't like not knowing, it annoyed me. I would just have to solve the mystery, then.

I crashed my lips down on hers, catching her by surprise, and drew a moan from her. She gripped my hair tightly to the point where I could feel her nails digging into my scalp. Letting my tongue tease the seams of her lips, I slowly brought my hands around her waist, down to her rear. I rounded them, feeling the soft warm flesh against my palms. I squeezed.

Amy moaned again, dragging me closer to her if possible. Finally when she couldn't breathe anymore, she pulled her lips from mine, sucking in a breath. "Your bed or mine?"

"Who needs a bed?" I picked her up and turned around, setting her on my counter. The thigh-length nightgown she was wearing was highly convenient as it easily allowed me to pull it up and access what I wanted. She allowed me to tug it off her body, exposing her to me. I let my eyes glaze over her body, taking it in.

Tan skin, pale breasts, creme nipples, hourglass figure, shaved from the neck down. Bottomless.

"You really came prepared," I noted tilting my head a little sideways, observing her breasts. They looked like D-cups. "Are you that confident in yourself or did you think I would be easy?"

"A little of both," She mused, a slight smirk tugging at the corners of her lips. "I know I can be beautiful when I want to be, and after all, didn't I get you here pretty easily?"

"You never got me, I got you," I said, grabbing her chin. "I think you'll quickly find that I'm not your average prey, Amy. I don't play games, I don't beat around the bush. If I didn't have the fullest intentions of fucking you right here on this counter, I wouldn't. The state of the matter is I'm bored and you're horny. It's that simple to me."

She bit her lower lip, dragging it between her teeth before exhaling. Her cheeks were tinted with arousal. "Then fuck me. Don't keep me waiting."

I hated waiting myself.

I brought my lips against hers again, grabbing her neck in the process. She met me with force and wrapped her legs around me while her hand reached for my tie. She untied it and tossed it on the floor before she went for my shirt. Without hesitation, she tore it open, letting the buttons fly everywhere. The next second she was dragging it off my shoulders. I allowed her.

Once my shirt was removed, I brought my hands to her breasts while hers planted against my pecs. Hungrily, I felt her fingers roam across the broadness of my chest, down to my belt buckle. My hands cupped her two reasonably large breasts and I weighed them, feeling her nipples harden against my touch. A soft moan escaped her lips as my mouth traveled down her neck. I could feel her hands working on my belt, unbuckling it, before pulling it out of my pants completely. It joined the rest of the discarded clothes on the floor.

When her hand unbuttoned my pants and slipped inside, she was met by my hardening cock. Stroking it softly, she released a moan as I returned the favor with a pinch to her nipples. She arched into me. "Russell... I can't wait any longer."

"Back pocket," I said against her neck. While her hands sought out my wallet, I let my teeth scrape and bite along the skin of her neckline. She tightened her legs around me, breathed heavily. She then managed to pull the condom out of my wallet and tossed my wallet away on the ground. She pulled back a little, reaching for my briefs. I allowed her to pull my pants down, taking my briefs with them in the process to release my cock. She laid eyes on me with a parted mouth, a small gasp escaping her.

I lost my patience. I snatched the condom from her hands and ripped it open myself while she seemed to be hypnotized by what was the simplest thing; a hard male appendage. I sheathed myself before grabbing her chin and turning her head upwards, forcing her eyes to meet mine. "There's time for staring later. Isn't this what you wanted?"

Her throat bobbed and she nodded. "Yes. God yes, I want this—you. I want you."

She then pressed her lips against mine again, hungrier than before, more eager. Her hands wrapped around my neck as I drew her closer, bringing her warm centre to my blunt.

And then I rammed into her with no warning. Amy cried out loudly and dragged her fingers down my shoulders. Her nails pierced my skin and drew blood. I gritted my teeth, groaning at the delicious sting of pain.

I had almost forgotten what it felt like to be welcomed in a warm wet cūnt. My ex-wife had cut off sex months before the divorce and I hadn't been a cheating bastard. It felt good finally being back in the game.

"Oh, God," Amy moaned, moving a little to adjust to me. "Shit, you're—"

I cut off whatever stereotypical sentence she was about to say by mashing my lips against hers. Slowly, I pulled out of her, only to thrust back in, impaling her. She mewled and arched her back. I repeated my action, picking up the pace just a little. I didn't beat around the bush, but there was no reason to cut to the chase. Not when this felt better than expected.

I let my lips travel to the crook of her neck again, sucking and biting onto her neck, leaving a trail of burning red skin. My hands found the rear of her ass, pressing her against me with every thrust. Each time, I felt myself go even deeper, hitting her where she needed it and where she could feel it most. Her moans grew louder and her words became incomprehensible noise. At last, I felt her walls tighten around me, grasping their release.

"Russell!" She screamed, probably waking up the neighbors both up- and downstairs as her ōrgasm overpowered her, leaving her spasming in ecstasy. Her nails clawed down my back and left a trail of scraped skin as I kept pounding into her. With a final thrust, my own release came, and groaning,

I let it go. My semen filled up the condom, warming her already burning centre.

"Oh, my God," She panted, clinging on to me. Sweat glistened on her body, rolled down the valley between her breasts and made her hair stick to her back.

Catching my breath, I pulled out of her, hearing her softly sag with exhaustion. I disposed of the condom in my trashcan after tying it in a knot. Behind me, I could hear her carefully getting off the counter, picking up her clothes. I myself pulled up my briefs and pants, buttoning them.

"Can I borrow your bathroom?" I heard her voice behind me. When I gave a nod, she trotted off to my bathroom and closed the door behind her.

A few minutes later, she came out again, fully clothed in her little nightgown, her skin still slightly flushed and her lips still bruised. She slandered into the kitchen to me where I had taken the liberty to pour myself a cup of the coffee I had brewed before what transpired. It was practically cold by now.

"I don't think I will be needing those batteries after all," She told.

I took the batteries into my hand, weighing them. "Take them anyway. I won't always be here when you need a fix."

She accepted them when I handed them over to her and then she looked down at them for moment. "Perhaps not. Thank you for your hospitality, Detective Crane. I hope to see you again soon."

With a last smirk, she then went to my door with a sore sway to her hips.

I kept drinking the cold coffee, staring at the door as she left, deep in thoughts.

I hadn't solved the mystery yet, but now I had gotten closer. She had suffered abandonment. That's why she felt so passionate about sex. She needed the closeness without the actual closeness. It was a survival technique mankind had invented which went back as far as the cretaceous period. The need to make love when it felt like nobody loved you. Once they had gotten their fix, their partner was trash to them.

Or, in Amy's case, a trophy. All the people who she had screwed but who never got the chance to screw her over.

And you just joined the shelf, my inner voice said.

The only difference between me and that Maddox guy, for instance, was that I didn't care. I could care less if she cared or didn't care about me. Love meant about as much to me as the numerous soap operas they aired on TV.

And that right there was why you got divorced.

"Detective Crane, always a pleasure," Ms Dee said, pursing her lips as I walked into the police station.

"It would sound so much more convincing if you didn't force your voice to sound so exquisitely polite, Ms Dee," I replied, giving her flat look. "May I suggest giving up on formalities in the future and instead just tell me why you called me so we can avoid these unpleasant encounters?"

Ms Dee pressed her lips even tighter together, grabbing the folder in her hand so tightly her knuckles turned white; I had that effect on most people. "After what happened yesterday,

I find myself in the need to keep a close eye on you if you decide to misbehave again."

"Misbehave?" I said, exasperatedly. "We are five years apart in age, Erika, let's not do the whole mother/son act. Find a husband, have a kid and then do it if you're so keen on playing house. Or, you could take the alternative option and look into BDSM. I heard that's making a comeback."

Ms Dee turned beetroot red and clenched her fists. "That is enough out of you, Mr Crane! I should fire you here and now if it wasn't because—"

"—because I solved your case last night," I interjected and held out the bloody murder file. "You're looking for a murder with a conscience. He murdered the victim with an axe as the autopsy confirmed, but got remorse which was why he left the 'sorry' note. Judging from the force of the stabs he used, to the distinct way he wrote the 'y' and the 'r' in the note, I'd say he's about 18-20 years old. Kids from that generation used a particular swing to their letters since the times and trends were changing. And, judging on what the witnesses described, he's most likely caucasian. If we take into account that he probably felt bad after having murdered whoever this person was to him, he would've hidden out somewhere in the slums of his neighborhood because he was too scared to go home. At that age, it's highly likely he still lives with his parents, and if they are somewhat good at their parenting job, they must have reported him missing by now. I would start there." I handed Ms Dee the case file which she with a small hesitation then took.

She cleared her throat. "Well then. You solved another one."

"Which is why I'm hoping the reason you called me down here was because you had a new case, and preferably one that's more exiting than this one."

She nodded, taking a deep breath to collect herself. "It is. Go see Leon about it, he just got back today. He has the file."

"In that case, enjoy the rest of your day," I said before striding past her. I started heading down the hall.

Leon Jones was about the only other detective who could stand working with me. I had worked with him for three years since my name got known by the police force. For some reason, he was sympathetic about me and my methods. He allowed me to do things my way and didn't stand in my way when I was on crime scenes. In a way, I think he saw me as his partner. He seemed to care about me and had on numerous occasions invited me home to meet his children and wife. That was back when I was still married. I hadn't seen him in almost two months though, since he and his family had been on vacation in Europe, visiting some family.

"Russ!" Leon greeted me once he saw me over the top of his cubicle wall. He was a six-foot-five African-American who honestly looked like someone who should be competing in the NBA's. "Good seeing you again. Did you make it into the new year alright?"

"I got divorced. Where's the new case?"

His smile immediately dropped and a serious frown replaced it. "Divorced? You and Janelle split up?"

"That is the meaning of the word divorce to my extend. The case, Leon. Dee said you had it."

Leon looked lost for words for second, before looking down at his cluttered desk. He started going through his files. "Shit, I'm sorry to hear. What happened?"

"My work finally got to her," I impatiently replied, waiting for him to find my case. "Said I wasn't home enough."

"You kept traveling back and forth between Kansas and Florida, you can't blame her on that," Leon paused his search, to my annoyance, to send me a pointed stare. "Did you ever consider taking some time off?"

"Did you ever consider cheating on Michelle?"

I watched as Leon's face grew hard. "You're playing unfair, Russ. Are you saying you'd rather choose work over a happy life?"

"My work is my happy life, now shut up and find me my case before I leave." I had never been so impatient to look at a grisly murder case.

"Here you go," Leon finally said, pulling a file out from the rest of them. "If you just had breakfast, I'd suggest waiting to look at the pictures. They're messed up, those fucking Russians. We caught one of them. He's in detention and he's all yours whenever you're ready."

I opened the folder and skimmed the case before going to the photos. Dismembered female, raped before murdered, according to the autopsy. She had been a prostitute and apparently she had gotten involved with the wrong crowd, but what had me hooked was why they killed her.

"She stole something from them. That's all we could get out of the Bratva guy we caught before he started cursing Russian profanities and hit a guard," Leon voiced as if reading the glow in my eyes. "It was real important shit apparently, and guess what? She hid it somewhere they don't know and now it's a race against the Russians. If we get our hands on it first, this could mean big things for the police. We've been fighting these guys for years, you know that. If whatever she stole were plans of something they were planning to do and we get our hands on it first... well, you get the idea."

I blocked Leon's voice out and studied the prostitutes face, the pictures from her social network profiles. She was wild... uninhibited... most certainly into BDSM. Purely looking at her updates, plus the pictures from her social network sites, she was a prime candidate for Sexual Masochism Disorder. Locked up in chains that strategically covered the sensitive parts of her body and whips held in her palm, she was a girl who enjoyed her pain. Yet somehow, I doubted that she enjoyed getting dismembered by the Russian mob.

Whatever she had stolen from them had to be something worth giving up her own life for. Something that meant something to her. She wouldn't bother stealing the Russians precious plans for some terror stunt. She was a prostitute, what good would those do her? She could sell them at best, but she was too smart to do something crazy like that. She had a nice education, good grades according to her school records. She wouldn't be dumb enough to steal just anything from them. No, this had to be personal... but why would the Russian mafia torture her like this, then? And what did they have in common? Where was the link between them, the bond that tied them togeth—

My eyes drifted down to her body, glaring at her pelvis.

Solved.

"Earth to Russ? You're spacing out again, man."

My eyes snapped and I closed the folder. "I solved it. That took what, five minutes?"

Leon's eyebrows shot to the air. "You solved it? Just by looking at the file for three minutes?"

"I didn't look, I saw. Contrary to everyone else who opened this," I snorted, waving the folder. "Did you even try to investigate from this?"

"Jesus Christ, just give us the answer!" Leon barked, standing up. "Where's she hiding the info she stole?"

"It's not about where she hid it, it's about what she hid," I say, throwing the folder down. "Young woman, mid-twenties moves to Florida to seek success. Something goes wrong, she ends up selling her body to strangers at night. A condom breaks, an accidental pregnancy, a baby is delivered—"

"Wait, hold up, how do you know she got pregnant?" Leon frowned, picking up the file and going through it. "There's no birth certificate and the coroner didn't mention anything in his report about her being—"

"Because it was years ago, but you can still tell on her hips and breasts," I said, taking the folder from him. "Look at the early pictures from her social network updates. Now look at the latest. Her hips are set wider, and that's not from being fucked sideways, that's from childbirth. Labor changes a woman's body—you should know, you have three kids."

Leon gave me a skeptical look, but then forfeited. "So what next?"

"The baby got taken from her; perhaps the authorities? More like the father showed up. Why would a woman—who has absolutely no gain from hanging with mobsters—suddenly seek them out? Perhaps because they had something of hers."

"Wait a minute," Leon interrupted, scrunching his forehead in deep thoughts. "Are you telling me that the mobsters stole a kid?"

"Splendid, you're keeping up," I sarcastically remarked. "So the woman seeks out her son, who—if we calculate from the date of the first pictures online and of the width of her hips, to the huge month-long gap where she didn't post anything, to the present date—is about five years old."

Leon scratched his chin. "But... what the hell does the Russian mob want with a five-year-old kid whose mom was a prostitute to them?"

"Finally you're asking the right questions," I said, turning on my heel and walking towards the interrogation room.

"Wait, Russ, where the hell are you going?" Leon called after me, scrambling to pick up his gun and badge. I heard his footsteps behind me.

"You said she had stolen from them and I just concluded that what she stole was her kid. A five-year-old," I snapped, turning a corner in the hall.

The realization was finally dawning on Leon and his black skin suddenly turned ghost white. "Holy Christ. Are you saying we have a missing five-year-old kid in the city that's being chased down by the Brat—"

"—I'm going to get that Russian speaking so fluently English, he'll be able to immigrate once I'm done."

CHAPTER 4

"**D**amn it, Russ, we told you not to provoke him."

"We got answers, didn't we?"

"But look at the damn cost!" Leon snapped at me, running a hand over his short afro. "I swear, if you could see yourself..."

I glared flatly up at him with the one eye that I wasn't currently pressing an ice bag over. "I don't care. I got you your answers. Mafia druglord Vahlov Pretikov is the father of that little boy. He needs an heir, takes the kid, momma fights back, daddy doesn't like it. Daddy teaches mommy a lesson, but mommy has already taught daddy one. Baby boy is gone and now starts the grand search for where mommy hid him. So, with that summarized, give me a new case before I get bored again."

Leon scoffed, leaning forward on his elbows. "I'm not giving you anything until I'm sure you're back on your feet. Take a break, Russ, what you're doing isn't healthy. On top of your divorce—"

"I'm sorry, am I crying right now? Use your eyes and make your own goddamn deduction," I snarled, wincing as I stood up. "I should hope that the Miami police hasn't completely lost the ability to make one, even if the evidence is compelling."

"Watch it. We give you a long leash to play, but don't go acting all shit on us for worrying about you," Leon protested, standing up. His six-foot-five beat my six-foot-three, but even then I didn't find him intimidating. "We're just try'na look out for your superior ass."

I rolled my eyes and reached for my jacket after ditching the ice bag on his table. "Then get me a new case before I die of boredom."

"If you ever need a friend, just call," Leon called after me, after I turned and walked down the hall. I didn't bother replying.

I left the station and headed home.

"What the hell happened to you?"

I glanced over my shoulder from my kitchen to the door of my apartment. Amy stood leaned against the sill, watching my bruised topless body. I saw a slight frown of concern stain her face.

"Monday's," I curtly replied, returning to cleaning the wound on my chest by the kitchen sink. When I heard her step into my apartment, closing the door behind her, I added, "Please come in."

I felt her hands on my back, running over my shoulders, down my arms. Her lips pressed against the nape of my neck. "What happened?"

Gritting my teeth, I clenched the sponge in my hand and kept my focus on the wound by my rib, not the fact that she was only wearing boxers and a white transparent T-shirt. "A Russian mobster took a few swings at me. Nothing serious."

"That," She said, poking my swollen eye, "doesn't seem like nothing serious. Did you ice it?"

"Yes."

"For how long?"

I turned around, catching her by surprise again and captured her in my arms. "Why do you care? Scared that one of your trophies got a dent?"

Amy glared up at me, pursing her lips. "You're not a trophy—"

"The hell I am. I'm another guy to your collection and you know it, so you can unclench. We're not dating and I'm not your boyfriend, so why are you really here?"

She glared, squinting her eyes a little at me. Then, slowly, she leaned into my ear and whispered; "You're the detective. You figure it out."

When she slowly leaned back,I did a take down her body; Boxers, white shirt, bare feet and exposed legs. I could smell her coconut shampoo and lotion, meaning she couldn't have showered more than an hour ago. She wasn't wearing make-up or anything else that could get smudged or ruined. Her hair was loose and she had deliberately put on a see-through white T-shirt before coming here. Her hardened nipples underneath revealed she wasn't wearing a bra. Even without this deduction, I could've said without a doubt in my mind that she came to get the void between her legs filled.

Meeting her eyes, I could see her getting aroused by the fact that she knew I just studied her.

"Why don't you just hold up a sign?" I said, leaning back against my kitchen sink.

"Because I like watching your eyes work," She smirked, stepping up to me, pressing a hand against my chest. "And reading is too boring for you, isn't it?"

She pressed her lips to my jawline and let her hand slide down my torso to the buckle of my belt. I closed my eyes.

Why do you let her do this? She's more fucked up than you, why do you keep sleeping with her?

I felt her hand slip into my unbuckled pants, rubbing my hardening member. I sighed. "Amy..."

"Come now, Detective Crane, what's holding you back? You were very willing last night."

My conscience, that's who's holding me back.

But then again, I never listened to it before, so why start now?

Gripping her hips, I brought my lips down on hers, meeting them with the same passion she offered. She moaned and leaned into me while still keeping her hand in my pants.

I pulled her hand out before picking her up and walking her to my bedroom. "You win, Amy."

"Why are we here, Leon?"

"Because I know you don't eat breakfast, so I thought I'd give you the opportunity to do so."

"Oh good grief, is this where I'm supposed to be flattered that you care? Because I'm really not."

"Enough, Russ, just look at the damn menu," Leon glared at me from across the booth at the diner we were in. According to their menu board outside, they served coffee, a delicious variation of breakfasts and sunny-side-up smiles. The annoying music they played in the background (which sounded alarmingly much like 80's music) was beginning to annoy me. Unfortunately that title had already been claimed by Leon who had refused to talk to me about the new information they'd gotten on the Russian case unless we got a bite to eat—and apparently Omeletta's Diner was his preferred choice.

"I don't eat while I'm working, digesting slows me down," I said, impatiently running a hand through my hair. I couldn't wait to get this over with. I had to be seriously desperate if I agreed to go to diners with police officers, just to avoid getting bored. I needed work.

"Yeah, and so does dying from malnutrition," Leon dryly added. "Just eat, will you?"

Gritting my teeth, I picked up the laminated menu card and skimmed it. Eggs, bacon, pancakes, omelettes, what a surprise. They served oatmeal, for crying out loud. "I think I'll stick to coffee."

"Christ, Russ, no wonder you got divorced if you're this difficult to dine with. When was the last time you spoke to Janelle?" Leon said, raising a brow of concern.

Oh, you have got to be kidding me. "If you wanted to question me about my failed marriage, a breakfast date wasn't needed, Leon. Not unless that breakfast involved a healthy dosage of heroi—"

"—finish that sentence and the only thing you'll be eating is the bullet of my gun," Leon cut in, slamming his menu down. "You quit a long time ago, Russ, don't start thinking about that again. Divorce is tough, and getting back in the game again—"

Dear lord, kill me. "I think I'll take that bullet now."

"I'm serious, Russ. If you need someone to talk to, you're always welcome at my house."

I glared flatly up at him, wanting to seriously just roll my eyes and leave, but he had my case—the thing I had resorted to as my fix instead of drugs—and without my daily dosage, I sure as hell would turn to my old friend Syringe. So, instead of leaving, I sighed, closed my eyes and massaged my nose bridge, trying to contain my irritation. "Thanks for the offer, but it's not necessary."

"Fine, but if you change your mind about talking about your divor—"

"Good morning, gentlemen, what can I get you?"

My eyes flew open and I glared up at Amy who stood in front of our booth in uniform and apron. Her face was straight, but her eyes were amused and trained on me.

"Good morning, Ms. I'll take a cup of coffee and one of your famous omelettes, please," Leon politely spoke, completely unaware of the tension between me and Amy. Then again, he had no idea I had spent last night between her legs, making her scream so loudly, the downstairs neighbor came up and asked if everything was alright.

"No problem," She wrote down on her little notepad before turning to me. "And you, sir?"

Her eyes glinted with humor as she spoke that last word sir, addressing me so formally. Last night she could barely form my name on her tongue from the brain-wrecking pleasure of climaxing so hard. You could tell she was enjoying watching me being caught off-guard.

"Just black coffee." I said, meeting her eyes. If she was expecting me to squirm, she could think again.

She scribbled it down before giving us—me—a glance. "Coming right up."

I followed her with my eyes as she walked back behind the counter, back to the kitchen to give the order. She looked over her shoulder, sending me a smirk, as if knowing I was staring at her.

"So as I was saying, if you change your mind, the offer stands. Michelle would be happy to take you in for a few days, you know how she loves cooking for more people, and my kids—"

"I'll be right back," I said, still glaring at Amy who watched as I stood up from the booth. "Bathroom."

Leon said something to me, but I didn't bother listening. I was heading down the bar, towards the kitchen, and evidently also the bathroom. Amy had turned to the coffeemaker, but the smirk on her face remained as she started pouring up coffee.

"You know, I don't believe in coincidences," I voiced, leaning in on my elbows on the bar. "But running into you here is making me rethink."

"Surprised? Why am I even asking; the look on your face was priceless," She mused, still keeping her back turned to me. "Does 'deer caught in headlight' mean anything to you?"

Funny. "How much did you hear?"

"Of what? Your conversation? Just enough to know that that finger you buried inside me yesterday used to have a ring on it."

"Who's eavesdropping now?"

"You did start," Amy finally turned around, holding two cups of coffee in her hands. She set them down on the counter in front of me. "I never got a chance to ask; Did it turn you on, listening to me moan your name when I masturbated? Maybe it's a little redundant to ask, considering what we've been doing the last couple of days, but I am still curious."

Her eyes locked with mine and I could just see the mischievousness glinting inside them. She was quirking her brow ever so slightly and tilting her head, toying with me. No deductions needed for what was on her mind.

I stood back up, unbuttoning the first button on my shirt. "Would you mind showing me the way to the bathroom?"

Her smirk only grew. "Certainly. Sir."

Fifteen minutes later, I was walking back to Leon who had been patiently waiting in the booth. I ran a hand over my hair to smooth it down before I sat down across from him again.

"Everything okay? You were in there a long time."

"My toilet visits, really? That's the topic you choose to strike up right before eating?"

He grimaced. "You're right, forget I asked."

I adjusted my tie a little, fixing my collar as Amy walked up to our table, looking a little flushed with her hair slightly undone and her cheeks still pink from minutes ago. In her hand she carried a tray with our coffee and Leon's breakfast. "Here you are, sorry that took so long."

"It's no problem, we aren't in a rush," Leon politely smiled, unfolding his cutlery as Amy placed the omelet in front of him along with our coffees. She didn't meet my eyes as she set mine down in front of me. "Thank you."

"No problem," She straightened her apron out and brushed a strand of hair behind her ear. "Call if you need anything."

"We will, thank you," Leon smiled and Amy smiled back before taking a step away. Our eyes quickly met and I couldn't help but smirk briefly as I saw the memory in her eyes sparkle with me taking her up against the bathroom door while she panted for her breath, trying to stifle her moans. She quickly looked away and left.

"You sure you don't want anything?" Leon asked me, cutting into his omelet.

I rose my coffee to my lips, taking a sip. "No thanks, I actually ate already."

Chapter 5

I hated waiting, it killed my brain slowly. It was waiting that led me to do things like drinking, doping, or in my most recent act of boredom, fucking my neighbor.

But, from what I could hear from the other side of my bedroom wall, Amy was busy, and in a way, so was I. Not with fiddling with whatever made so much metallic noise inside her apartment, but with something far more delicate and probably better tasting.

A bottle of Bombay.

I was lying in my bed, contemplating whether or not I should open it. Leon could call any moment and say they found some locations to scout. Maybe some new evidence. Or maybe even found the missing kid, though that one was highly unlikely. They wouldn't find that kid without me, that was for sure, and that was also partially why I hesitated opening the bottle.

But I wanted it. Really badly, in fact. I usually wasn't the person to hesitate; I either did something or didn't do something, and then I was done with it. Big shit. But, drinking while working on an abduction case with a kid as the victim... if that wasn't careless, then what was?

I heard something metallic creak from the other side of the wall, which was followed by the sound of Amy's sudden loud outburst; "Sonofabitch!"

Something hard thumped and then the door went. I waited exactly three seconds before I heard her footsteps outside my door. And then came the knock.

I closed my eyes for a long second before I got up. The universe sure had a fun way of keeping me from drinking.

I opened my front door and was met by a very soaked Amy; Her hair was dripping and the front of her shirt and the beginning of her short were drenched in what looked like dirty water. My deduction, along with the metallic sounds I had heard from my room, told me that she had a faulty pipe.

"Do you know how to fix a sink?" She said after the initial eye contact. My first reflex was always to read the other persons body first before reading their eyes, but Amy was always upfront.

I crossed my arms, doing another take of her wet persona. "Do you?"

"Clearly not," She snorted, wiping a droplet of water away from her forehead which had been moving down to her eye. "Can you help me, please? I need someone to fix my pipe and I don't mean that as a euphemism. I'm having company later and it wasn't meant to be a pool party."

I sighed and looked down at the floor for a second. Fixing a sink was better than emptying a bottle. "Fine."

"Thank you."

We walked into her apartment—me for the very first time—and I took a good sweep of her home with my eyes.

Stuffy, bohemian, a little messy. Not that I was an expert, but most women usually like their places nice and welcoming. Especially those who were supposed to have company later. Amy's apartment was not.

It revealed that whoever was coming to visit clearly wasn't someone she held high opinions of. Not enough to clean her apartment, but yet still just enough for her to make her bed, which was there, right when you walked in. There were less than five feet from the bed to the door, showing that she didn't waste any time at all. Once prey had been lured into her apartment, prey was already caught in the web.

But I wasn't prey today.

When I turned my head to her kitchen which was past her sleeping area, across from her tiny living room, I saw her sink leaking water and was forming a big pool on the dark wooden floor.

"It has been leaking all week and this morning I got tired of emptying buckets," She said, wiping her forehead with her arm. "I decided to try and tinker with it, but clearly my middle name isn't Tinkerbell."

"Mine isn't either."

"No?" She combed her fingers through her wet hair. "What is it, then?"

"Isaac." I walked up to her sink. Water was still gushing out.

"Isaac? Detective Russell Isaac Crane," She slowly said. "I dare you to say that five times fast."

"Wrench."

"Excuse me?"

I turned and gave her a flat look. "I need a wrench."

"Oh," She said, dropping her crossed arms. "I thought you were calling me one. Hold on." She walked up to her shoe collection which was pushed together in a cluster on the floor. After searching for a moment, she pulled a wrench out of one of the boots. "I got pissed off when the pipe snapped and then sprayed me, so I hurled the wrench away. Here you go."

She handed me the wrench and I took it, laying down on the wet floor in front of her sink. I then turned the valve which stopped the water from flowing.

"Oh. Smart idea," She grunted. "Well, looks like you got that under control. I'll go take a shower then, if you don't mind."

I just kept working on loosening a few bolts on the sink that seemed rusty. After a moment when she realized I wasn't going to reply, she sighed.

"Alright. Have fun, then."

I wouldn't exactly call it having fun, but I would definitely call it keeping me from becoming an alcoholic again.

About twenty minutes later, Amy came out of the bathroom with a trail of steam following behind her, which spread to her entire apartment and engulfed it in a fruity scent. She had a towel wrapped around her wet hair, but had for my benefit (obviously) omitted the towel around the rest her body. This allowed me to see her naked body in all its gorgeous womanhood. Right from her peaked nipples meeting the cold air, to her long slim legs, to her slick pussy that still was slightly moist from the shower. And freshly shaved.

I took back my previous statement; I was indeed prey today as well.

"Take a picture, it lasts longer," She smirked as she walked up to her dresser and picked out her clothes. She went with a red thong and a bra to match, along with a girly, flowery summer dress as her attire for the day. Not her usual preference of wardrobe.

"Not in my head," I replied. "Pictures can burn, be misplaced or torn up. I found my memory is better at storing data than physical objects."

"Am I data to you?" She wondered while slipping on her thong.

I rose a flat brow at her. "Am I not just another dick to you?"

She pursed her lips thoughtfully for a long moment as she strapped on her bra. "I suppose you make a fair argument, Detective. How's the sink coming along?"

I had long ago turned my attention back to the steel pipe above me and gave the last nut a good twist. I then turned the valve back on so the water could flow. "Try turning on the tap."

She walked over to me, smirking down at me as she strategically placed a foot on either side of my body so I had the perfect view of her pussy. She then turned on the tap, letting the water flow. For a moment, it seemed to flow easily and untroubled.

- And then the pipe burst again, spraying dirty water all over me, much like it had done her.

Amy quickly turned off the tap, just as I turned the valve and blocked the water again. I ran a hand over my face, removing the residue droplets on my face. "You have a rusty pipe. You need to buy a new one."

Amy stepped away and allowed me to get up. "Fantastic. That's just what I needed," She sighed and unwrapped her hair from the towel. She handed it to me. "I'm sorry about your shirt... though I must admit not too sorry."

She smirked as I took the towel and dried my own hair off, which much like hers, was soaked. The same thing applied to my white dress shirt and I guessed that was the reason Amy didn't feel too bad; I imagined this had to be right out of an erotic novel to her; the handyman getting soaked in his ever white shirt so she could see through to the muscular frame beneath.

I felt like rolling my eyes purely from the ridiculous and nauseatingly cliché scenario.

"You can dry off in my bathroom," She said, sighing heavily after a moment of staring. "I need to mop up all this water before I get company and you dripping on my floor doesn't help. Go," She said, making a simple nod with her head towards her bathroom. "But don't take too long, my guest can be here literally any moment."

"I live right on the other side of the wall. I can dry off there."

"Aren't you even the least bit curious about who my guest is?" She now asked, cocking her brow as she begun to pull on her flowery dress.

"No, I already know who's coming."

"You do?" She said, actually surprised.

"You're trying exceptionally hard to impress someone," I said, stepping closer to her. I watched as she narrowed her eyes. "You don't have a single piece of flowery fabric in your house, not even as much as a green plant, yet you have a summer dress with alarmingly pink roses on it, and it just so happens to look new. Judging by your constant fidgeting and the way you keep glancing around your apartment, you're worried about what your guest might think of your place, maybe even yourself, yet for some reason, you want to give off the appearance that you're not trying so hard, which is why you didn't bother stacking your shoes properly or vacuuming the floor. You however did make your bed," I noted, glancing over her shoulder to her bed, before looking back at her. She gulped. "There's only two distinctive groups of people that other people make their beds for. The first one is obvious; lovers," I said, raising a brow. "But you never bother with that, do you? You know that most men you bring here are already so impatient to be inside you, they don't care if your bed is made or not."

Amy gulped again and looked down at my lips. "You're not impatient right now."

"I'm not most men."

She looked up at my eyes again. "So what's the second, then?"

I cocked my head a little to the side. "I don't know about you, but there's only one person in my life that cares if my bed is made or not. I'm guessing it's the same with you."

Amy glared stunned, but then blinked. Just as she was opening her mouth to stutter a reply, there came a knock on her door. It startled her so much, she made a high-pitched yelp. I stood quietly as she blinked perplexed before she quickly rushed over to her door. Her eyes left mine as she swung it open and greeted her guest.

I thought I had guessed who would walk through that door. My obvious deduction of her room had been that she was expecting a family member—her mother to be exact. And while my deduction was incorrect, it wasn't totally off, though.

None other than Amy's older sister stood in the door and smiled superiorly down at her. Her hair was slightly darker, her skin was a bit fairer, but her features looked a few years older. Everything right from her finely manicured French tips to her polished makeup and hair, not to mention the lint-rolled, ironed business suit she wore, told me she was the older, accomplished sister. And she was obviously here to gloat on her little sister.

Amy's behavior suddenly made sense.

"Hello, Amy," She said, stretching her smile a little wider at her sister's sloppy, unfinished appearance. "Am I too early? We did say 10am, didn't we?"

"Yeah, you're punctual as always and I'm running late as always," Amy replied, a muscle in her jaw twitching. "Come in."

Her sister walked in with her cocky grin, but immediately froze when she saw me. A deep crease formed between her brows and grew deeper for each second she looked at me. "I'm sorry, who is this?"

Amy closed the door behind her and slowly walked up to her sister. "This is Russell Crane, he's my next door neighbor.

He was just here helping me fix a pipe," She said, gesturing to the wet floor.

"Oh, I see," Her sister's smirk immediately returned to her face as she did a take of my body.

I enjoyed watching it happen, seeing her own petty, inconclusive deduction take its judging shape on her face; She saw my bare feet, the ones that probably looked dirty now, thanks to Amy's unwashed floor. She saw the dirt splotches on my faded black pants, maybe even saw the small, worn-out mark by my pocket from where I kept my phone. She looked at my drenched white shirt which at least was buttoned correctly, but probably looked wrinkled the places it wasn't wet. She saw my jawline, the chin I hadn't shaved in two days, and she saw my eyes which had dark rims beneath them because of sleep deprivation.

In her eyes, I was poor, unemployed, sloppy and unintelligent.

Amateur.

"Pleasure to meet you, Mr Crane," She said, giving me a nod instead of a handshake.

I continued drying off my face and neck while not providing her with a nod back. "You're welcome."

She gave a stiff glare and turned to look at Amy. "I thought we were going to be alone today."

"Like I said, Russell was just here to help me fix a pipe," She replied, giving me a look that told me to confirm it. I wasn't going to do that. I was going to do something much better.

"Yes, I'm sorry about the mess, Amy did tell me she'd have company," I replied, looking her sister in the eyes. "I'll just clean it up and then I'll be out of here."

"Oh, you don't have to—" Amy begun, but I cut her off.

"It's okay," I said, giving her a pointed stare. "You wanted my help, now you got it."

Amy pressed her lips together for a moment, before giving up. "Alright. You don't mind, do you, Irina?"

Irina, as her sister's name had to be, gave a vague shrug before she sighed. "Well, it's your place. Speaking of which, those drapes you have over there, they block out too much sunlight. It's so... depressing in here," She said, stepping further into Amy's apartment. "You should reconsider those."

"Right..." Amy tiredly said, walking up to her closet before pulling out a mop for me. "Here, thanks again, Russell."

"No problem."

"Oh, so you do have a mop," Her sister chuckled. "I thought your floors were so dirty because you couldn't afford one, but I guess you just didn't have time to do it, did you?"

I discretely glanced sideways and saw a muscle ticking in Amy's jaw. "No, I didn't. I just came from a night shift at the diner actually, so I'm a little tired."

"Oh, of course, I know how you feel. George works so late at the hospital that when he gets home, he's too tired to cook, so of course I do it for the family," She chuckled again, walking around the apartment, looking at everything and nothing. "I just put down the lawyer's briefcase and strap on the apron."

Amy was losing her cool and I could very well understand why. She kept clenching her fists and unclenching them for each piece of propaganda her sister spewed; She was telling her that she was working harder than her and that she still managed to do the house chores such as cooking and cleaning. The stuff of a real suburban wife.

And like every suburban wife, she had her secrets; Secrets I already had spotted from the moment she stepped through the door.

"Would you like something to drink?" Amy offered, her voice sounding strained. It was obvious her polite tone was forced. "I have ice-tea, milk, water—"

"Obviously," Irina clucked, looking towards the water on the floor I was patiently mopping away. She then glared at me like I had just disturbed her thoughts. "I think ice-tea is fine."

Amy sent me an apologetic look, even though she knew I brushed her sister's judging stare right off me. That sort of pettiness didn't touch me even the slightest. But it touched Amy.

While she poured her sister some ice-tea, Irina took a seat in one of her wobbly wooden chairs. She rested her purse in her lap and started fiddling with her wedding ring. "So, Amy, how's the single life these days?" She asked which only made me have to hide my smile. "Are you seeing anyone?"

"Which question do you want me to answer?" She asked a little defensively as she set the glass of ice-tea down in front of her sister and took a seat across from her. She had also poured a glass for herself which she slowly sipped.

"The last one," Irina replied, grimacing at the worn-down glass Amy had given her. "Have you found a proper boyfriend or are you still living life vivaciously with different men?"

Amy squeezed her own glass so tightly, I considered if she was going to break it. After a moment, though, she eased her grip and set it down. "Nope, no boyfriend. I'm still promiscuous."

Her sister sighed exaggeratedly and folded her hands. "I do wish you could find a nice man and settle down, Amy. You're not going to stay young forever, you know."

"I am aware of that."

"I just can't stand to watch you so... miserable," She said, glancing around. "You need a man in your life."

"FYI, I'm not miserable, and not everyone needs a man to survive," Amy finally said, breaking the cold surface of her anger. "Just because you're married and living the perfect suburban life doesn't mean I'm living life wrong."

"I never said you were doing wrong," Irina gaped in shock at her sister's sudden burst. "I just meant, maybe you should make some changes in your life, like..." I could feel her glancing sideways to me where I was finally getting done mopping the water up. "Maybe you should change the circle of people you hang around."

Amy's eyebrows shot up. "You're passing judgment on me based on my neighbors? That's cute, Irina, act like you know me."

"I wasn't—-" Irina quickly said when Amy shot up and walked up to her sink with the glass, past me. I met her sister's shocked eyes. "I'm sorry, Mr Crane, I didn't mean to—"

"Yes you did, and it's okay," I spoke up, leaning on the shaft of the mop. "You're entitled to your own opinions. After all, this is a free country."

She frowned a little, but then gathered her composure and straightened up. "I'm happy you see it that way, Mr Crane."

"Oh don't worry, no offense taken, Ms...?"

"Mrs Jefferson," She sharply corrected me with a little cocky smile. "I'm married."

"Really? That's interesting," I said, frowning theatrically. "I guess it makes sense, though, because from the way you keep fiddling so nervously with your wedding ring, I would hang onto the word Mrs as much as I could, too."

She blinked perplexed and dropped her jaw. "E-excuse me?"

"It's a giveaway," I said and pointed to her ring. "Either you got married a few weeks ago and still can't get used to the feeling of a wedding ring on your finger, or you're having marital problems that's causing you severe stress. The most common thing to do when one is stressed or under pressure is to fiddle with something; The page of a book, a loose twine, a pen, or in your case, your wedding ring," I mused, cocking my brow. "I wonder if your marital problems are in any way linked to your deep-seeded need to seek out your sister and point out her flaws every now and then. One could almost think you do it as a sort of reassurance to prove to yourself that no matter how bad your life is, it's still better than your sister's. It makes you feel good about your own crappy existence knowing your sister is doing much worse than yourself. Of course that leads me to the question if you even really should consider yourself a good person, or even more importantly, a good sister." I watched how each word I spoke pulled another shade of color out of her face until it was as pale as a ghost's. She opened and closed her mouth so many times, eventually she had to clear her throat.

"H-h-how d-did you—"

"I'm not finished. If you're going through a tough time, it could just be a way of surviving, putting all your frustrations onto your sister. Your need to criticize her is linked to your own need to look so polished and clean," I said, now walking closer. "But no matter how spotless and clean you present yourself, it's always a splattered, colorful self-portrait. For example, the way your thin black pencil skirt has been closely picked from any spec of dust could be affiliated with wanting to show off a professional, clean look. You're a lawyer, obviously it's important to show authority."

Irina gulped down a little and seemed to regain some color. "T-that's right, it's expected of me."

"Exactly. It's expected of you from work," I said, emphasizing the last word. "But since today is a Saturday and you clearly knew you didn't have to fight to outshine your sister, you still decided to strap on your best suit. Why? Maybe because Mr Jefferson hasn't been looking at you too much lately," I said, stepping even closer. "Maybe he's been working more than late hours, and maybe you know he's cheating, and just maybe, that's the real reason you asked your sister about the single life. Not to gloat on her unaccomplished victories concerning the partnership between a man and a woman, bur because you're failing that yourself and you have a feeling that soon enough, you'll be riding that vivacious single-life train right along side your little sister."

Her eyes were wide, her mouth was open and her bottom lip was quivering. She was glaring at me like I was the Devil in disguise and I was here to crush her. Which I was.

Because what kind of sick person got a kick out of coming here with the fullest intentions of bringing her own sister down when she was already struggling enough as it was? I might have been an inconsiderate prick at times, but right now in this room, I wasn't the biggest one. Even after my harsh speech, Amy's sister still took the crown.

"Who the hell are you?" She finally snapped, glaring venomously at me. "How dare you research—"

"He didn't research you, Irina, it's what he does," Amy confidently said, coming up to me. "He's a detective who works with the Miami police. He deducts for a living."

"And I also know how to mop a floor." I added with a sharp look at Irina. I then turned to Amy and handed her the mop. "Are you good from here?"

"Yeah, I'll do," She nodded. "But I think me and my sister need to talk more privately now."

"Indeed," I agreed. I turned then turned to her sister who still seemed too shocked to speak. I gave her a brief nod, just like she had given me. "Good luck with the divorce, Mrs Jefferson."

CHAPTER 6

For the next hour or so, I heard a lot of yelling and shouting coming from the other side of my bedroom wall. Amy was blowing out all the frustrations she had obviously kept caged inside her for years, while her sister was calling her names and shouting out all her flaws. True family as I knew it.

In the meantime I had buried myself in my work again. Even though I knew I never missed a clue, I kept going over the details of the kidnapping.

One thing bugged me; Vahlov was no amateur when it came to killing, yet he left the body in the wide open city for us to find it. He could've gotten rid of it, burned her corpse, and he wouldn't have had the police sniffing around his case. The kid's mother had been a prostitute with minimal family. Nobody would've reported her missing, at least not for months, which at that point the trail would've gotten too cold to investigate. Who cared about a street prostitute these days?

So why did he leave her for us to find her?

I heard the sound of final words being said on the other side of my wall before a door was thrown open and then slammed shut. I heard something breaking—a vase or a glass—against the door before Amy's silent sobs begun. The bedsprings of her mattress creaked and I now knew she exactly what she was doing. She was trying to bury the pain with what she knew best; Pleasure.

I focused my mind back on the papers in my hand, going over the pictures taken at the murder scene of the dismembered prostitute. There had to be something I had missed, something obvious, right in front of me...

Three short knocks sounded on my door. My head slowly rose and I looked at it. I knew it was her.

Standing up, I walked out of my bedroom and over to it. I opened the door and looked at her. "If you need a shoulder to cry on, forget it. I don't do tears."

"I don't need a shoulder to cry on," She said, meeting my eyes as she stepped closer. "I need a dick to ride on."

I sighed when she put her hands on my chest, grasping my shirt. "The vibrator not enough this time?"

"Not after I had you. I only want you now," She whispered, stepping onto her toes. She gently pressed her lips to mine and I kissed her back.

"What about Maddox?" I said between kisses, cocking a brow at her as I wrapped my hands around her waist. "I'm sure he'll be more than willing if you purr enough into the phone."

"I don't want Maddox, I want you," She said again, gripping my shirt tighter. She begun dragging me out of my apartment, into the hall. She cleverly managed to close my door behind me, locking me out. I didn't care.

"I can't fix you," I told her when she pulled me into her own apartment. I lifted my hand and trailed my finger across her jawline. "I can give you a fix, but I can't fix you. I live with trouble."

"I know," She murmured, looping her arms around my neck. She closed the door to her apartment with a small push and then continued leading me to her bed. "That's why you keep coming back to me. I'm trouble."

"You knocked on my door."

"But you never say no." She leaned in and pressed a long, deep kiss on my lips. I kissed her back, traveling my hand down her spine. After another moment she pulled away, breathing heavily. "You want me as much as I want you."

I gripped her shirt, pursing my lips a little. "We share similarities, Amy. We both don't do love and that's the only reason I'm here right now. That, and it keeps me from dwelling in boredom."

"Oh, just say you like my pussy." She ran her hands through my hair. "It's so much easier."

I gripped her hips and pulled her closer to me. She exhaled shakily as I grabbed her chin with one hand and turned her head sideways. Bringing my lips down to her ear, I whispered; "I like your body; Not just what's in between your legs. How often does Maddox tell you that?"

She turned her head to me, her eyes dark. She bit down on her lip before she pulled me closer and brushed her lips against mine. She kissed me hard and I met her with the same force.

From there on, all bets were off. Amy ripped my tie off, unbuttoned my shirt while our tongues mingled. Not moments later, we were on her bed, tangled in her sheets.

She sat on top of me and rode me while her hands rested on my chest. Her hips swayed sensually as she tilted her head backwards, getting lost in the sensation. Beads of sweat were rolling down her forehead and chest, casting a luminous glow onto her skin. Her breasts were round and heavy, her nipples dark and peaked. Her slender, supple waist thinned in at her stomach, but her hips were womanly, curvy and full. Just like her lips.

"Why do you let your sister intimidate you?" I asked, feeling her inner walls clench deliciously around me.

"Because she's my sister," Amy breathed. "She's always been the good one, the perfect one. Everything she does is golden in our parents eyes. Whenever I do something, I'm a disgrace to the entire family."

"Sounds like a nice family," I sarcastically commented.

She looked down at me and frowned. "They are my family. They're all I've got in the world."

"What about Maddox?"

She moaned softly as she languidly rode me. "We dated for a while, but I'm horrible at relationships. I get bored with the same old dick, so I cheat. Every guy turns out to be a real shithead. No one can satisfy me. Not like you do."

"Stop trying to coax me into believing I'm the first proper lover you've had, we both know it's a lie," I said, sliding my hands up her smooth thighs. "We also both know you're a nymphomaniac. You enjoy and survive on having sex with multiple different partners. It's what you do."

"What I do, is fuck," She said, thrusting down on me hard, making me grunt. She leaned down to my lips and hovered just above them. "Sex is the best thing in the world, so why not do it all the time with whomever you see fit?"

"And here I thought love was the best thing in the world," I retorted, putting a sarcastically demeaning emphasis on the word 'love.'

"I don't believe in love," She whispered against my lips. "It's a chemical reaction in the brain that gets activated in certain situations, but like all drugs, it never lasts. So I fuck."

I looked at her for a long time while she sat back up again and began riding me harder, faster this time. "What the fuck are you doing flipping pancakes in a café, Amy?"

"I'm not, right now I'm riding your cock." She leaned down to suck my nipple into her mouth. I closed my eyes for a moment, salvaging in the feeling.

"You're smarter than you look."

"And you're sexier than you know. Ever considered trading out the tie for a pair of sunglasses?"

"Sunglasses block my vision and I need my vision," I clenched my jaw when she moved up the tempo, the squelching sound of our sexes colliding increasing. My hips started meeting her thrusts, puncturing her deeply each time her pussy swallowed me.

Amy begun panting, digging her nails into my chest. "Yes... you do. Everything... you do... depends... on... your eyes..."

"Not everything," I replied through gritted teeth. I could feel her inner walls begin to spasm around me, tightening in an ōrgasm that was bringing my own closer. "There are other ways to deduct. Sometimes, it all about... the feel."

Amy combusted in her ōrgasm, sobbing into the ceiling as she rode it out. Her nails dug into my chest and drew blood as she claw her way down my torso. That cut the last shred of control I had before I felt myself release and spill into the condom. Amy collapsed on top of me, panting heavily, just as I did.

"That felt amazing," She finally said when she had a breath to spare. "So amazing."

"Feeling better about your sister?"

"Yeah," She whispered, still panting heavily. "There's no way that her uptight husband fucks her this good."

"That's what happens when you get married," I closed my eyes, simply just breathing. "The ring forged in fire ironically enough kills yours."

Amy sat up a little and took my left hand, watching where the little white tan-line around my ring-finger still showed the telltale sign of the wedding band that once sat there. "How long were you married?"

"Six years."

"Were you the one who ended it?"

"No, she did," I replied, braiding my fingers with hers. "My work got in the way like it always has for the women I've dated."

"How old are you exactly?"

"Twenty-eight."

"So you got married when you were twenty-two?" She said, raising a brow.

"I could get you a calculator if you want to double-check that."

"I'm twenty-four," She volunteered. "And I'm not looking for anything serious."

"I know you're not, if you were, I wouldn't have let you seduce me."

She smirked a little, then tilted to the edge of the bed and padded around on the floor with her hand until she found whatever she was looking for. It turned out that thing was my phone. "I'm putting my number in," She smiled, opening my phone and begun clicking on the keys. "If you get too lonely, give me a text or a call." She hit Save before shutting my phone again.

I raised a flat brow. "I don't get lonely. I get bored."

"Alright, then if you get bored," She smirked. "You'll have something to do."

I just closed my eyes again as she kissed my chest, letting her tongue twirl out to tease me. "It's your own mistake, Amy."

I woke up, not even realizing that I'd fallen asleep. I was still in Amy's apartment, the afternoon light streaming in through her windows. I tilted my head slightly to the side and found her awake, watching me.

"What?"

"I've just been watching you sleep." She replied and smiled a little.

"Oh, for Christ's sake, get a life." I snapped and rolled my eyes. I then brought my hands up to rub some life into my face.

Suddenly I heard my phone ring from somewhere in her room. Turning away from her, much to her dislike, I patted around with my hand on the floor before finally finding it under her bed. Sitting up on the edge of the comforter, running a hand through my hair, I tiredly pressed answer. "Crane."

"We got a possible murder suspect here at the station, but he's not talking." Leon's gruff voice said on the other end. "We caught him lurking around the station, trying to scope up some 411 on the case."

"Russian?"

"Looks like it, but as I said, he ain't talking."

"Describe him to me. Age, height, weight, ethnicity, clothes, everything."

"He looks like he's in his early twenties, about six foot two, Caucasian, but dark black hair. Brown eyes, fairly buff for his age. He's wearing loose camo-colored pants and a black ripped shirt with some logo on it. Converse shoes, worn out. Leather jacket, ripped. If I didn't know any better, I'd categorize him as the stereotypical bully of any normal high school."

"And you got him into the interrogation room?"

"Yeah, didn't put up much of a fight. He's been there for two hours, still hasn't let out a peep."

"Are you there right now, watching him?"

"Yeah, I'm on the other side of the glass. Why?"

"Are his hands folded on the table or resting in his lap, and is he looking around or looking down?"

There was a small pause wherein I guessed Leon studied the kid. "Hands are folded on the table, but he's looking down. Why?"

Feeling Amy crawl up behind me, gently pressing her hands to my shoulders, I closed my eyes. "He's their fall-guy. They sent that kid to take the fall for the murder, but he's as innocent as the high school bully you described. The way he's sitting shows that he's surrendering, but he's scared. Hands on the table shows he submits, but the way he's looking down means he's scared. If his hands had been in his lap and he had been looking around, he had been there for trouble. Inverted, but daring you to make a move on him. This kid is not, he's just there to take the blame. Release him. The biggest stains you'll find on his police record is graffiti, I guarantee it."

Amy started kneading my shoulders and pressed small kisses up my neck while I waited for Leon to reply.

"That's crazy, man. We just got a hit on his fingerprint. Mikhail Rocoff, 22, Russian immigrant, no more than a few DUI's and a dozen vandalism charges."

"Put him back in school and tell him to tell Vahlov, I'm disappointed," I scoffed. "Sending a minor to take the fall for his dirty work and expecting me to fall for it? That's an insult to my intelligence, I deserve better than that."

"Come down to the station and tell him yourself," Leon snapped. "Why aren't you at work yet?"

"I was under the impression that you called when you needed me. I'm not leaving unless you actually got something."

"Oh, we got something, and this is a 10, Russ. You're gonna wanna see this."

"What is it?"

"Let's just say, you've got mail."

Pressing my lips together and furrowing my brows, I replied. "I'll be there in 20." I hung up and threw my phone back on the floor.

"I love when you do that," Amy murmured against my neck, still massaging my shoulders. "Deduce."

I stood up and turned around, catching her hands and braiding my fingers with hers. "That's called being sapiosexual." I leaned down to her lips and kissed her, drawing a shudder from her. "You get aroused by intelligence."

When she moaned, I knelt down on the bed and cupped her face. I made sure to kiss her slowly, like I was fucking her mouth with my tongue. I felt goosebumps rise on her skin and the pulse in her neck beat faster.

"Do you have to go to work right now?" She whispered against my lips.

"Yeah, I do." I replied, meeting her mouth again. I let my lips travel down the canyon of her breasts before cupping them with my hands. "They need me."

"I need you."

I pressed a kiss on each swell before observing them. They fit nicely in my hands. "No, you don't. You had me earlier and now I'm going to work. You can use one of your toys if you're desperate, which judging on these," I pinched both her hardened nipples which made her moan and lean her head back. "you are. So get to work."

Releasing her body and standing up again, I heard her whimper in frustration before she plonked down on her bed. I started going around her room, picking up my clothes that in the frenzy earlier had been scattered everywhere. My tie was hanging on a lampshade.

"When will you be back?" She said, reaching in between her legs to tease me with the sight of her playing with herself.

I indulged her. "When the case is solved."

She slowly licked her lips, arching her back as she slipped two fingers inside her soaking heat. "Will you come fuck me when that happens?"

Fixing my tie, I kept my eyes on her. "We'll just have to see, won't we?"

And with that, I left her apartment, after grabbing my phone, and headed down to my car. A cold shower would have to wait until I got to the station.

~~~

"Is this what you call professionalism?" Ms Dee quipped at the sight of me walking in to the police station in my wrinkled clothes. "Have you looked yourself in the mirror?"

"I haven't looked myself in the mirror for ten years, it's a waste of time," I ran a hand through my tousled curls. "What's the news?"
~~~

Her eyes sharpened at my dry reply, but at least she didn't comment any further. She knew in a battle of having the last word, I'd win. Even if she was my 'boss'. "Leon has it, go get briefed from him. He's in his booth."

Without answering, I strode past her, heading for Leon's cubicle. I found him bent over his table, frowning seriously at his computer.

"Where's the mail?" I asked in a voice that I could only describe as offensive. I didn't care at this point.

When he heard my voice, Leon looked up. "Good, you're here."

"You called me."

"And I promise I did it with good reason," He darkly said, clenching his jaw. "Take a look at this."

I came into his booth and glared at his computer screen. It was a video file pasted into an email, with the subject line; 'FOR DETECTIVE CRANE.' Pursing my lips, I glared at it. "Mind pressing play?"

Leon pushed a button on his keyboard and the video begun. It was a dark room, but you could just see the contours of a person lurking in the shadows.

"Roses must wilt, but only after the seed has planted. Only then can it ensure its legacy on this beautiful earth—only then will its roots continue to grow."

That was a thick Russian accent if I ever heard one. Speaking in fluent Russian, Leon of course had no idea what he was saying. But I did.

"I have never been a fan of roses, Detective Crane. Even as beautiful as they are, they always carry thorns. You can cut them off, but roses are a stubborn plant, even if it is fragile. They sprout new thorns and eventually become impossible to handle. It's better to let them wilt or to cut off the stem."

"What's he saying?" Leon whispered when Vahlov held a pause. I silenced him with a single finger.

"This rose is mine, Detective Crane, and I fully intend to keep it while it's still blooming. Anyone who tries to take it from me will get their stem cut. I think you'll find I am a skilled botanist. You have been warned."

The video ended and I pursed my lips again, resisting the urge to smirk. That had certainly been insightful.

"What did he say?" Leon repeated, a little more impatiently. "Did he speak about the kid?"

"He spoke in sloppy metaphors, but essentially he told us to back off—me in particular. He finds me a threat to his beloved mafia and its inheritance."

"Inheritance? As in... he wants his kid to take over for him?" Leon, asked exasperatedly.

"I thought that was redundant to say at this point. Why else do you think a mafia lord would adopt the one-night-fling bastard child he got from a prostitute's sullied hands? I hardly think his biological clock chimed in if you catch my drift."

"Alright, so Mafia lord takes kid to get an heir," Leon needlessly summarized. "Where does that leave us?"

Smirking, I crossed my arms. "It means we gotta break out the weed whacker before the weed kills the seed."

CHAPTER 7

"The kid, Leon," I snapped. "I've been so focused on the details of the murder, I forgot to pay attention to the actual missing kid. It was his plan all along. He distracted me with a blatant murder to keep me distracted from what was really important."

"Which is?" Leon said, frowning. "Are you saying you made a mistake?"

"Not a mistake, I just jumped to conclusion too quickly," I replied, whipping out of my chair, pacing the floor. "The kid, Leon! I just assumed it was a boy, but it wasn't. It's a girl."

"Okay... so we have a missing girl on our hands?" He frowned, confused. "What does it matter if it's a boy or a girl?"

"Everything," I drawled impatiently. "Good God, I'm surrounded by incompetence."

"Watch it, Russ. Just get to the point."

I sighed exasperatedly, trying to prevent myself from exploding. This was good. Really, really good. Of course I hated the fact that I had been so blind, but it was nice to finally have a real challenge.

"In the video Vahlov talked about gardening; roses in particular," I begun, looking at Leon's nonplussed face. "He spoke the sentence; 'Roses must wilt, but only after the seed has planted. Only then can it ensure its legacy on this beautiful earth, only then will its roots continue to grow.'" I recited. "Do you get it now?"

"Humor me and elaborate."

I rolled my eyes. "For God's sake, he's talking about the kid! The 'seed'? That's the girl! The rose, that's her mom, our victim. Vahlov learns of her pregnancy and takes the kid from her. I only assumed he did that because he wanted an heir, and based on the how backwards things work in the mafia business, I just assumed it was a boy," I explained. "A man like him is most likely to choose a son take over his business once he's dead, not a girl. But not this time."

"Slow down, how did you even discover it was a girl and not a boy?" Leon questioned, still desperately trying to keep up. For Christ's sake, it wasn't that hard. I wondered how dull the world had to be in his eyes.

"By what he said in the end," I impatiently continued. "This rose is mine, Russell Crane, and I fully intend to keep it while it's still blooming," I recited again. "He talked about the kid's mother as a rose in the first part, and here he used the same feminine approach to refer to his kid. He wants to keep her while she's still blooming," I slowly said, as if Leon was retarded. "So that he can spread its roots—he wants to keep her so he can one day eventually use her as a bargaining chip for a marriage between two cartels; Spread its roots; Their roots."

Leon just stared. "You got all of that just from one metaphor?"

"Vahlov is smart," I smiled to myself. "He's really smart, in fact. And, he's a 'skilled botanist.' He knows how to nurture a fragile rose into becoming a very beautiful, pliant one."

"So to summarize," Leon said, furrowing his brows. "The kid is a girl. Vahlov intends to keep her until she's grown up, at which point he wants to marry her off to another drug lord to expand his cartel?"

"Congratulations, you followed. They should put a medal on you, too," I sarcastically drawled.

"Quit it, Russ," Leon growled. "We aren't all arrogant, knowledgable pricks."

"I'm not asking you to be arrogant, just knowledgeable, which after more than 12 years of schooling shouldn't be too much to ask for, but apparently, I am mistaken."

"Alright, that's enough," Leon barked, standing up as well. "Did Vahlov give any hint as to where the kid might be?"

"Not other than the obvious he already mentioned, which was probably the easiest understandable piece of information he gave us," I said, rolling my eyes.

"Russ, for Christ sake—"

"He has the girl! 'This rose is mine and I intend to keep it'. Find Vahlov, you find the girl. That's about as fucking clear as it gets!" I yelled, furiously running my hands through my hair. "Go call your supervisors, tell them to check out all of

Vahlov's known cartel locations. Be useful for once in this investigation."

"I should punch you to the ground," Leon growled, taking a threatening step closer to me.

"That would be a considerable waste of time, considering there's a little girl currently in the claws of Miami's biggest crime lord. Go find her before he fucks her up and she ends up in a mental hospital for the rest of her life."

Leon gnashed his teeth, but as a father of two girls and one son, his priority switched to finding the little missing girl. He turned away from me and picked up the phone on his desk.

"One last thing," I said.

Leon glared over his shoulder, pressing the phone to his ear. "What?"

"The girl's name is probably Rose."

I was back in my apartment, going through all the case files one more time, this time broadening my focus. I wanted to make sure I hadn't missed any more vital clues, because if I did, Vahlov got one step ahead. And I really hated falling behind.

I had spread all the files out on my floor and my coffee table in the living room, save for a few which I had hung on the wall. I started to connect the pattern, trying to see the bigger picture.

A fix would've been good right about now, my inner voice desperately reminded me. That rush of energy, the clarity it brought to your mind...

"Fuck off," I growled, closing my eyes.

"I can come back later, then?"

I whipped around and within second had Amy's innocent persona pinned beneath me on the couch, my hand clutching around her neck. Once my mind snapped out of its fluke, I realized I was choking her.

"Christ, what the hell are doing here?" I snapped, quickly letting go of her. Amy gasped for her breath with a mortified expression, heaving in air. She coughed and placed a hand over her throat.

"Jesus!" She squeaked. "Are you insane?!"

"You snuck up behind me and I've put away serial killers with a good memory and delicate taste for vengeance," I flatly replied. "I've learned to be on alert."

"Maybe you should begin locking your door then," She coughed a little again and sat up. "I just came to check up on you. You've been locked up in your apartment for two days."

Had it been that long? I didn't take notice of that kind of thing. When I was working, I was working.

"Are you okay?" She asked and looked at all of the files spread on my floor, coffe table and pasted on my wall. "Is this just one case?"

"You know I can't discuss that with you," I said, getting up from the couch. "I'm hungry, I'm going to order takeout. You want some?" When she didn't reply, I turned around and found her smiling. "What?"

She looked at me and then shrugged. "It's just, one minute you're tackling me on the couch while talking about murder cases, the next moment you're doing something as ordinary as ordering takeout. I find that a little amusing. Is your life always so wildly swinging back and forth between normal and catching a killer?"

"I try to keep it on the catching-the-killer part, but every now and then I'm forced to entertain myself with normal things like food," I dryly replied. "It's so very tedious having to attend to basic needs when there's a world of mysteries waiting to get solved. Unfortunately, the world can't keep up with me, so I end up getting bored and doing—"

"—me," Amy finished for me. She smirked. "I think I'd like that takeout now, and afterwards, let's see if I can you get bored."

"Yo, Russ, wake up."

Opening my eyes, blinking in the harsh morning light, I focused on Leon who was standing in my bedroom. "What the fuck?"

An amused grin stretched on his face as he glanced towards Amy who was naked and sleeping on top of my chest, backside uncovered. I angrily cursed under my breath before yanking up the covers to shield her body. "What the hell are you doing in my apartment?"

"I came to check why the hell you weren't picking up your phone." Leon replied while Amy slowly started to stir, her sleep getting disturbed by our conversation. "Didn't know you had company."

Rolling my eyes, I rubbed my face, trying to rid it from all signs of insomnia. "Get the fuck out of my apartment, Leon."

"I will, I just figured you'd be interested in this." Suddenly he pulled a manila file out from under his jacket.

Amy finally woke up and snapped her eyes up to Leon who in his leather coat looked somewhat like a thug. The damn idiot.

I ignored her timid stare and sighed. "Is that a new case? Otherwise I'm not getting up."

"It's an old case that never got solved. I think you're going to love this one," Leon chuckled, sending Amy a smile. "But just for the record, you're still on the Russian case. This is just to keep your head busy while we do our job."

"Who is that, Russell?" Amy asked, wrapping my covers closer around her body.

"Colleague," I answered, finally sitting up after she retracted to her side of the bed. "Who's leaving the room so I can get dressed."

"I'll be waiting in the kitchen. You got coffee?"

"Knock yourself out."

I threw my covers off and stood up, pulling on my briefs from last night once Leon was out. I hoped whatever case he brought me was good. Otherwise he was going to be the one getting punched to the ground. I could tell by the amused grin on his face, he thought I had found a new girl. How majorly disappointed he would be when he learned the truth.

"You're going back to work?" Amy said behind me, spreading out on my bed while I got dressed. She lifted her legs seductively at me while lying on her stomach.

"You heard Leon," I replied, pulling on my pants. "They got a case for me."

"Do they turn you on? The mysteries?"

I paused, midway through picking up my shirt from the floor. Instead I stood back up, facing her. "I make my living off solving puzzles that no one else knows how to solve. You see a new male neighbor and you think target. What does that tell you?"

She rose a brow at me, yet at the same time pursed her lips. "It tells me that we both chase what's wild and new, and in the end, we both get our climax. And yet... you still let me into your bedroom after solving a case. What does that tell you, Detective?"

I glared down at her, picking up my shirt. "Everyone's gotta do something to fill the boredom."

"So I'm just your plaything?"

"Aren't I yours?" When all she did was glare at me with her mouth half open, I lost my patience. "I gotta go. I trust you can find your way back to your own apartment."

I left my bedroom, closing the door behind me. Distracting my brain from what just went down in there, I focused on Leon who was sitting in my barstool, reading my old news papers I hadn't even opened.

"Damn stupid politicians," He grunted, turning a page. "Trump needs a reality check."

"You said you had a case," I flatly interrupted, pulling on my shirt. My chest was scratched down by Amy's claws, mildly bleeding as I stretched, opening some of the wounds. "Either present it or be presented to my hallway."

Leon closed the newspaper and dug out the file. He threw it down on the counter in front of me. "Let's see how fast you can solve that one."

I picked up the file, opened it and begun reading. In my peripheral vision I could see Leon studying me, obviously wanting to say something about the woman in my bedroom whom I could hear was making her way to my bathroom. After another two minutes of reading the file, I finally snapped. "What?"

Leon looked amused and sipped his mug of coffee. "Isn't she that waitress from the diner?"

"Sharp deduction, Detective."

"She's not what I pictured as your type. Especially after Janelle."

"She's not my type," I said, giving him a hostile glare. "I don't have types."

"Alright, so what are you doing sleeping with her? Is she your girlfriend?"

Closing the file with a wham, I threw it back on the counter. "She's my neighbor and she's a nymphomaniac. I sleep with her because I get bored, and this," I said tapping the file, "Is bullshit. If you can't solve this one by yourself, then I pity you and the entire police force."

Gnashing his teeth, Leon growled. "We aren't all geniuses, Russ. Solve this one and we pay nicely. Now spit it up."

I scoffed, running a hand through my hair. "You've got to be kidding me. Read it again if you've even read it at all."

"Watch it," Leon glared, picking up the file. "You're on thin ice."

"Read it."

"What am I looking for?" He replied, scanning the page. "We've been over it a hundred times."

I needed a drink. A strong one. "How delightful it must be having your brain, tell me; is it fun being completely incompetent?"

"Russell!" Leon angrily snapped, standing up.

"A duke with a precious gem that's been hidden in a secret vault behind a painting gets stolen without setting off the alarms," I barked, punching a fist into my table counter. "He has three daughters, all of which are the prime suspects because they all knew where the gem was hidden and what the combination for the safe was. All three daughters were questioned, but none of them charged since their stories were inconclusive."

"Exactly, so what's the answer to the puzzle?" Leon snapped. "No one else knew it was there, his wife is deceased and nobody else lives in the manor. It has to be one of the girls."

"It is." I said, taking a deep breath to calm myself down. "The gem was reported missing last summer. It says in the file that this duke lives in northern England, yes?"

"Yeah, so?"

"My God." I sighed, leaning my head back, glaring at my ceiling. "Did you read the three daughters testimony?"

"Yeah, the daughters got questioned and all three said they had been in the study that day when the gem was stolen," Leon said, looking down at the file with a frown. "The first said she went to borrow a book, the second said she needed to fetch her fur-coat, the third said she had been watering the plants for the maid who had been sick that week."

I pinched my nose bridge, closing my eyes. "The answer is right in front of you, Leon. It should be even clearer now than back then, six months ago."

"Just give up the answer, Russ," He snapped, sticking out his jaw. "Stop prolonging it and spill."

"This case is from six months ago," I said, gritting my teeth. "Florida might have humid sunny weather all year 'round, but England is covered in snow right now because it's January."

"What does the weather have to do with anything?"

"Everything!" I shouted at his incompetence. He seriously hadn't figured it out yet. Nobody had. Humanity was lost. "Six months ago, England wasn't covered in snow," I said, walking over to my door, sliding my feet into my shoes. "They had sunny weather like we do right now, even if England isn't know for its warmth. They. Had. Summer."

"For Christ's sake, just say it!" Leon roared, slamming his fist on my counter, too. "What's so important about it being summer in England six months ago?"

I grabbed my car keys, fixing my eyes on Leon, as I opened my door. "Who needs a fur coat in the summer?"

CHapter 8

I had now after three more days grown tired of waiting for the police to scope out Vahlov's cartels, so I took matters into my own hand. I searched the police database for the last known locations he had been known to bag up cocaine and took a cab there myself. But, like every half-decent cartel, they moved just about every week or so. The places I went were deserted and held no trace of ever hosting legal activities. At least to the inattentive observer.

I crouched down in the abandoned warehouse I was in and picked up an old, dirty rag with small rainbows and stars on. It looked innocent enough, but of course it wasn't. I twirled it in my fingers before sniffing it. No particular scent, but it was covered in a dried, crackly substance I recognized; Snot.

This belonged to the little girl Rose, as her name had to be. Despite his words, Vahlov didn't seem like a skilled botanist, so why use this particular category of metaphors to deliver his message? There were hidden messages tucked everywhere inside it, and one of them had to be her name. Rose.

I stood up again, discarding the rag on the ground. I continued to walk around some more, kicking away a few planks of wood and turning over some old plastic covers that concealed old tires, junkyard crap and so on. No matter where I went, what I turned over and what I picked up, I had the constant feeling I was being watched. And I let them. If they were watching me, that meant I was getting close enough for them to have to keep an eye on me.

After a long day of walking around in abandoned buildings and construction sites, I finally headed back to the station. When I walked in, Leon was waiting for me.

"Tell me you did not go out to an abandoned drug house without me."

"If it'll spare your heart of the agony, I shan't," I replied, walking straight past him to the coffee stations, just as my pocket buzzed. I fished out my phone and saw that it was yet another text from Amy. She had been texting me practically nonstop with witty and sarcastic messages that usually held no dear information to man other than the fact that she was immensely bored. This text was yet another one of the same old meaningless prattling.

I'm starting to think that old phone of yours doesn't know how to receive texts from iPhones—maybe I should try sending a dove with the same message and see which one gets to you first? My money is on the dove - Amy

I rolled my eyes and shut my phone again.

"Russell," Leon gnashed. "I'm serious. Don't make me point out all the reasons why you shouldn't be alone in an old drug den."

"I won't, so you can rest your vocal cord," I replied, pouring myself a cup of coffee, just as another text buzzed in. I didn't even bother checking it this time. "I am more than capable of controlling myself, even if there were anything left at all for me to snort."

"I didn't know you had a sense of humor," Leon scoffed, not even a least bit amused. "Because that's hilarious. If I were to put a bag of coke in front of you right now—"

"—you would be the absolute worst cop on the planet," I said, sipping my coffee. I begun walking down to his cubicle. "Handing out cocaine to civilians? You'd put the entire department to shame."

"Very funny," Leon monotonously replied, just as I felt another buzz in my pocket. "Who is it that keeps texting you? Is it that waitress? What was her name again?"

"Amy." I replied as we took a seat in Leon's booth. He sat back in his chair while I leaned up his desk. "She programmed her number into my phone and I guess she must have programmed mine into hers as well."

"Who is she exactly?" Leon questioned with a raised brow. "How did it happen? Did she just knock on your door and boom, instant connection?"

I scoffed. "After three years I'm truly disappointed you don't know me any better." I felt another buzz in my pocket. "I don't feel a connection with people. I stay above getting emotionally attached."

"I don't know how the hell Janelle managed to convince you to marry her or why," Leon grunted, crossing his arms. "Are you going to reply to those texts?"

"No, and what do you mean 'you don't know how Janelle convinced me to marry her?'" I snapped. "I was the one on bended knee, holding out that big compound of minerals that women want on their finger. Last time I'll ever do that."

"Always the romantic." Leon noted.

Finally my phone begun ringing and angrily I stood up and answered the phone, seeing Amy's name on the screen. "I really sincerely hope this isn't one of those 'why aren't you replying to my texts' calls."

"Russell," Her voice was barely a whisper and she sounded scared to death. "There's someone inside your apartment. I-I think they're burglars."

I instantly whipped around and glared at Leon who sat up at my rapid action. "Where are you, Amy?"

"I'm in my apartment, but I can hear them moving around inside yours," She whispered, her voice shaking. It sounded like she was trying not to sob. "Oh God, I hear smashing, t-they're ruining all your stuff—"

"Stay where you are, I'm coming," I firmly said. "Don't move. Actually, don't even as much as move a muscle. The wall between our apartments is extremely thin. If they hear you shuffling around in there—" I cut myself off when I saw Leon giving me a lethal glare, telling me to stop scaring her and shut the fuck up. "Just stay where you are, I'm coming."

"Hurry," She whispered, her voice cracking.

I hung up the phone and grabbed my keys, already bolting towards the door.

"I'm coming with you," Leon said, also standing up. "Lemme' just call the squad and we'll—"

"No. No police, and you're staying here," I snapped. "I'm going on my own and that's final. Follow me and I'll tell your wife about the time you drunkenly kissed another woman."

"Russell!" Leon bellowed, but I had already bolted off. I was in my car before the minute even ran out.

I looked around my flat, stopping dead in the door that had been broken down; It was a mess.

I didn't own much, but what I had was scattered out on the floor everywhere. My books, my old files, my clothes. My one towel, my box of useless trinkets was turned upside down and smashed. My couch was tipped over and ripped up, my nightstand broken with a sledgehammer. My mattress was knifed. My laptop was destroyed.

Smirking, I crossed my arms. Finally. This was good.

"Oh, my God," Amy's shaky voice suddenly said behind me. She peered inside my apartment, timidly. "They broke everything. Russell, I'm so sorry."

I ignored her and kept glaring at my apartment. My clothes was torn up, my bathroom mirror was broken... I could see glass shards on the floor as well—my shower stall was probably smashed, too. They were pissed.

"Russell? Russell."

I held up a hand to silence her and took a further step into my apartment. Something crunched under my foot and I looked down. My coffee mug.

"Should I call the police?" Amy carefully asked, placing a hand on my shoulder. "I-I know you work with them, that's why I contacted you first, but I—"

"I got it," I said, reaching into my pocket. I dialed up Leon and waited two rings before the reply came.

"Talk to me. What happened?"

"There was a break-in, alright." I said, looking around to my smashed apartment. "Real mess. Everything's smashed."

"Christ. What did they steal? You have insurance, right? Did you keep any money packed away in there?"

"That's the thing..." I said, turning to look at Amy. "Nothing got stolen."

Amy frowned and Leon went quiet in the other end.

"Nothing stolen?" He finally said, exhaling heavily. "Possible robbery, but they didn't find anything they liked, so they just left?"

"So you think they broke in, looked around and saw nothing they wanted and then figured 'but let's trash this place before we go?'" I sarcastically snorted. "Come on, Leon, think. It's elementary."

The line went quiet again while he thought, and I used that time to study Amy. She was chewing on the inside of her cheek and was tipping on her feet. Anxious. Distressed. Scared.

"Shit, Russell. You shouldn't have provoked that mobster. I knew something like this was going to happen." Leon snapped, sounding exhausted with the paperwork that would surely follow after this break-in.

I scoffed, unimpressed. "The Russian mob is pissed about that, sure, but it's not enough for them to look me up and trash my apartment. This was a warning," I said, smirking while clenching and unclenching my fist. "I'm getting close, Leon, and they're telling me to back off."

I could practically see Leon frown deeply before my eyes. "Russ, I swear, if you're smiling right now—"

I hung up the phone and looked at Amy. She was still tipping on her toes, looking uncomfortable in her morning robe and white slippers. She finally spoke after minutes of debating whether or not she should. "Is the Russian mafia after you?"

I pushed my phone back in my pocket. "Not yet. They will be if I keep poking around."

"Then stop poking," She shakily said.

"That's never going to happen."

"Jesus, Russell, are you insane?" She snapped, wrapping her morning robe tighter around her skinny frame. "They're mafia! They have guns and drugs and—"

"—and a five-year-old girl who's mom they raped before killing," I interrupted. "A break-in doesn't scare me, if anything it thrills me. They just proved that we are getting close and they're not liking it. If they thought they could scare me away—"

"It scares me!" Amy cried, now shaking obviously. "I was on the other side of that wall! I heard them bust down your door, I was so scared they were going to break down my door too, and-and—"

I shut her up by pulling her into my body. She immediately broke down against my chest while I wrapped my arms around her, stroking her hair.

Good job, Detective. You managed to think of absolutely everything except for the woman you're fucking. Pat on the back.

"Amy," I said, rubbing her back. "I'm sorry they scared you. Don't waste your tears crying over them."

"I'm not crying about them, I'm crying about you," She sobbed, balling my shirt up in her fists. Her tears stained my tie. "I'm scared for you, Russell. What if one day you disappear because those mobsters got you? There'll be nobody to solve the mystery because you're dead."

I pressed my lips together, avoiding the words I really wanted to say; I don't care if I die. I wasn't going to say that, though. "Fear is intelligence in the face of danger, Amy. I'm not the one who should be scared and neither should you. The police is onto them, and with my help, they'll find that kid."

"And then what?" She whispered, sniffling. "The Mafia will come after you and they'll kill you for finding that girl. You can't win this one."

"What's the alternative? Leave that girl to be raised by the mobsters and wait 15 years until she's the one running the cartels?"

"At least you'd be alive another 15 years."

I pulled back, turning away from her, even if she tried to keep me there. "We are all going to die some day, Amy. Whether it be tomorrow or 15 years from now, it doesn't matter. We are all living corpses, just waiting to go to our grave. Why not die for something good?"

"Dammit, Russell, you don't get it do you?" She cried. "I care about you! You can make whatever deductions you want on how I look and what my appearance may tell you, but you can't deduce my heart! I'm scared for you," She whispered again. "I don't want to lose you."

I turned back around, granting her a look. "You barely know me, Amy."

"I know just enough about you to know you're a decent man," She said, wiping the tears away from her cheeks. "You're brilliantly smart, Russell. You have a gift, but its left you cynical and unattached because you're even more afraid of getting hurt than I am!" She now shouted. "You've made so many deductions about me, so allow me to repay the favor; You're a hypocrite! You say you have no interest in a relationship, yet you don't decline whenever I offer a warm body to hold. You might say you don't do love, but you were once married, and despite your effort to hide it, I can tell you miss her," She said, licking her lips from her salty tears that were now falling again. "I'm not her and I'll never be, but for now I'm a good replacement to you. I don't mind being one, because I need someone, too," She said, hiccuping as I slowly begun walking closer. "It's obvious we both have demons we try to suppress, but despite mine being the most obvious ones, you're still the one with the biggest shadow. You might act like you don't care, but you do," She cried, looking at me. "You do have feelings, so stop pretending you don't."

When she was finally done speaking, I took the liberty to softly embrace her and hold her in my arms. She accepted my comfort and sniffled against my shirt.

I slowly stroked her back, hearing her breathing even out. "Are you still scared?"

She nodded meekly, curling her hands to her chest.

"Would you like me to comfort you?"

She looked up at me, that look in her eyes. Wide, scared, yet her pupils expanded. I could tell what she needed, and I was more than willing to give it to her.

I leaned down and kissed her, letting my tongue swipe across her lower lip. She softly moaned, grabbing my tie.

Without much navigation needed, I pushed her backwards out of my apartment, closed my door behind me, then led her backwards into her own apartment, turning the knob. As soon as we were in, I kicked the door shut, my mouth never leaving hers for one second. I had her down on her bed the next moment where she wrapped her legs around me and mewled.

The next hours, as a gentleman, I could not divulge.

And yet...

"Aah, Russell!" Amy cried my name and met my thrust with her hips, throwing her head back into the pillows.

I kissed the valley between her breasts, keeping my one hand tucked under her body, the other one cupping her breast. I pushed inside her again, drawing another moan from her.

Her hands sought out my blond curls, burying her fingers into them, pulling. Sweat shone across her collarbones and down her breasts, along with the glistening trail of what I had done to her with my tongue. Her nipples were like knives in the air, begging me to kiss them, bite them. I did.

"Russell," She breathed, arching her back. "Yes..."

My eyes were focused on her breasts, the feeling of her warm centre clenching around me. With one final, deep thrust, I felt her climax.

"Russ!" She cried loudly, throwing her head back in ecstasy. I felt her inner walls spasm around me and felt her grip on my hair tighten. I watched her face as she ōrgasmed, listened to the sounds she made. As it finally subsided, she grew limp in my arms. She breathed heavily, eyes closed.

"Feeling better?" I asked her.

Her eyes slowly opened and she looked at me, a crease forming between her brows. "Why didn't you—"

I pulled out of her, getting to my feet. "I don't need it. Not today." I removed and discarded the empty condom in her bin. "Can I borrow your shower?"

Amy looked like she wanted to say something, but knew that if she did, she would get shut out. Instead she lowered her gaze to her bedsheets and silently nodded.

I stepped into her bathroom, turned on the water and stepped under the cold spray.

Focus. Stop thinking and focus.

I gritted my teeth and tried to force myself down, but my thoughts wouldn't leave me alone.

You put her in danger. You scared the shit out of her. No amount of pleasure you give her is going to make up for that.

You have to end it with her. Whatever it is you have, you have to end it.

Letting out a frustrated sigh, I gripped myself. I stroked my length, hoping it would make it go away faster. Perhaps jerking off was my only choice right now. The cold water wasn't even helping me.

I heard the door to the bathroom open, and in my peripheral vision, I saw Amy walking in as naked as I'd left her. When she opened the shower stall, I closed my eyes. "No, Amy."

"Yes," She countered, turning on the warm water. I felt her hand still mine and take over. "Let me do this for you."

I watched as she knelt down in front of me, letting the warm water wet her body and hair. Her hand softly stroked my member, making it harden even more.

I squeezed my eyes shut, running a hand over my face. What the hell was I doing?

Her mouth came around my blunt tip, ripping a throaty groan from me. Her tongue swirled out and tasted me; This was going to be torture.

Her head dipped. Once. Twice. Thrice. I stopped counting and instead gripped the top edge of the shower stall with my hand. My other hand found the back of her head and followed her movements.

Why was I doing this? Why was I letting her do this? I was suppose to end it, not lead her on. This was most certainly leading her on.

She took me in so deep, I felt my crown reach the back of her throat. I let out an involuntary groan and gripped her hair. "Shit."

Her pace quickened, pumping me with her mouth, swallowing me, making me nearly lose control. Nearly. I could feel my sac constrict as she sucked. This couldn't happen.

I pulled out of her at the last second, turning away from her as I erupted. I cursed, nearly breaking the glass with my fist as my semen splurted to the tile floor while I rode it out.

Don't. Lose. Focus.

"Russell..." Amy's hand softly landed on my shoulder, squeezing it.

I turned back around, and without further ado, clutched her into my body. I held her so tightly I probably hurt her, but I couldn't relax. I buried my face in her neck, breathed slowly but heavily.

I felt her arms come around me, run through my wet hair, before rubbing my back. For a moment, we stood like that while the warm water started to go cold again.

"I have to stop seeing you." I finally said. My words were muffled against her neck, but I was certain she heard me. Her body stiffened.

And then she surprised me by saying; "I know."

Letting go of her, I pulled back. "You can't come to me anymore. You can't even know my first name. Only my last, the one that's on my door."

She quietly nodded, and I was thankful she had the brain to know why.

"I'm going to step out now," I said, looking down at her sunken face. "And then I'm going to leave."

She nodded again and didn't object when I did as I told. I dried myself off, got clothed, and then left. And I didn't look back.

CHAPTER 9

Leon punched me so hard my vision blackened for two seconds.

"You goddamn piece of shit!" He roared.

Blinking my swimming eyes, I tried to focus on him, but it was no use. Even after getting punched, I still felt completely hazed. "Nice to see you too, Leon."

He yanked me to his face by grasping my shirt and glared murderously down at me. "You said you quit. Ten months, Russ. Ten. Months. And now after two weeks of no connection, you've gone back to this. You fucking disappoint me."

He threw me back on the ground in the abandoned parking construction I'd cooped myself up in, my back meeting the concrete floor. I groaned a little and tried to sit up. "Forgive me if I don't live up to your expectations. My first priorities are accomplishing my own."

"And is this what you expect from yourself?" Leon picked up an empty syringe on the ground with a tissue. "Doping yourself up until you kill your soul?"

"Technically, you can't kill—"

"Dammit, Russ! What happened?" Leon demanded to know. "Is this all because of the Russian case? I told you, you shouldn't have gotten in so deep—"

"Do you honestly think I'd dope myself because a gang of mobsters trashed my apartment? That would be a waste of fine medicine."

"What did you take?"

"Where's Michelle? Does she know you're out scooping addicts off the paveme—"

"What did you take!"

Leon's outburst echoed throughout the parking house. I glared flatly up at him. "Cocaine."

"You are a pathetic piece of shit," Leon seethed, dragging a hand over his short afro. "You have an amazing talent, Russ. I cannot believe you'd throw it all away on something as useless as drugs. Look at yourself, for Christ's sake!"

"I, am, not, an, addict." I spelled out for him through gritted teeth. "I'm an occasional user of pantothenic acids. It helps broaden my mind—"

"I'll broaden your goddamn mind!" Leon shouted, yanking me up to my feet by my shirt. "I really want to smash your head against the concrete if it wasn't because we need you! I'm taking you to a hospital so you can get a pump-out."

"Oh, for crying out loud, you are overreacting. I didn't even take that much."

"How much did you take? You know what, save it," He snapped, yanking me along. My body was too weak to protest. "Tell it to the nurse."

"Russell, it's so good to see you again," Michelle, Leon's wife, greeted me as soon as I stepped into their house. "Even though it's under such circumstances."

"And what circumstances are those, exactly?" I snapped as Leon closed the door behind us. "Getting forced to go to the hospital or getting forced to stay here for the night?"

"Pleasant and polite as always," She mused, giving me a smile. "I'm sorry to hear about your divorce."

"Why?"

"Because you and Janelle were a great couple, no matter how ludicrous it sounds in your ears." Michelle replied. She then turned to her husband and offered him a smile. "Hey, honey. I trust everything went alright?"

"Define alright," Leon scoffed, referring to the moment where I one-upped a nurse with my, quote; 'brain-talk'. "I'm just glad it's over."

"Me too, that was awfully tedious," I added, exhausted. "That nurse was incompetent, did you notice the buttons on her shirt? They were—"

"Begin that talkin' again and I'll send you right back to the hospital with a broken neck," Leon warned with a death glare.

"Hey!" Michelle sternly snapped, placing her hands on her hips. "I want none of that talk in my house. Behave your-selves."

I closed my eyes tiredly, rubbing my face while Leon muttered a sorry to his wife and gave her a quick peck on the cheek. It reminded me how much I didn't miss the marital life.

"Mr Crane!" A young voice suddenly chimed from the stairs. I opened my eyes and found all three of Leon's children running down the staircase towards me. Brilliant.

"Mr Crane!" Their oldest, Lea, who had to be about 15 now, smiled happily. She'd had a crush on me ever since I picked her up from school once. Once.

"Lea," I tiredly said, not bothering with offering a smile. I think it would only hurt her infatuation with me.

"It's so good to see you again!" She smiled and blushed a little once she stopped in front of me. Her siblings were right behind her. "H-how have you been?"

I gave a look to Leon who's eyes challenged me to even mention the drugs and the Russian murder case. "I've been good. Nothing out of the ordinary."

"We heard you got divorced," She said, a little nervously. "We're so sorry."

"Oh yeah, that. I forgot. That was four months ago, let's not linger in the past."

Leon cleared his throat besides me and I fought the urge to roll my eyes. Apparently he preferred lying to his children instead of being upfront with them. Or at least he preferred I did.

"Hi, Mr Crane," Their younger daughter Sara carefully said from behind Lea. She had to be around 11 now.

"Hello, Sara," I said, giving her a nod. "You've grown two and a half inch since I last saw you."

She giggled a little, nervously fiddling with her purple dress. "Mummy says I'm getting taller each day."

"Well, all normal humans between the age of 0 to 25 have been proven to grow each—"

Leon cleared his throat again, a little louder this time, and I gritted my teeth. His kids nervously glanced at their dad who gave them a reassuring smile. "Excuse Mr Crane, he's a bit tired."

"That's an understatement."

"Russ."

I rolled my eyes and instead focused on their youngest kid JJ, who was about 6. He was the spitting image of Leon, whereas Sara and Lea had taken on Michelle's features. He was shy and was partially hiding behind his mother. "Hello, JJ."

He shyly covered himself behind Michelle who chuckled a little. "Come on Jackson, say hello to Mr Crane."

JJ shy mumbled a silent 'hello' before he disappeared into the living room. Michelle rolled her eyes. "I'm sorry about that, he's very shy these days."

I yawned behind my hand. "Don't care. Since you decided to bring me here Leon, I hoped you prepared a bed for me. Otherwise I will have no problem returning to the—"

"We did prepare you a bed," Leon cut in, sending me a warning glare. "In the guest bedroom. Lea set it up."

"I closed the blinds for you, just like you like it," Lea quickly said, smiling nervously.

"That's sweet of you to remember, thank you."

She started blushing at my seemingly harmless compliment, and I could feel Leon scorching me with his gaze in my peripheral vision. He cleared his throat for the final time before straightening out. "I say we let Mr Crane get some sleep before dinner. He looks like he could use it."

"And a shower," Michelle noted, eyeing up my one-week-old clothes, greased hair and stubbled jawline. Not to mention the reek of gin around me. "I expect you to clean yourself up before we eat."

I grunted indifferently. "Can I go sleep now?"

"Come on," Leon sternly said, leading me upstairs.

"So, detective," Michelle smiled, handing me a glass of gin before taking a seat next to me. "How are you really doing?"

I took a large sip of the heavenly alcohol and swilled it around in my mouth for a moment before swallowing. I then leaned my head back against the couch and exhaled, exhausted. "I'm doing exceptionally well, considering I haven't been working in two weeks."

"Bullshit," Leon contributed, coming into the living room as well, holding a beer. He took a seat in the lounger across from me. "We know you've been scoping out the cartel's old warehouses in the brief intervals you didn't dope up."

I pursed my lips and swirled the gin around in my glass. "I was mainly trying to keep my brain alive since you cops don't have the foggiest clue as to what you're really dealing with."

"We do, Russ. We might not be you, but we do."

Scoffing, I took another swig of my drink. It was after dinner and the kids had been put to sleep. Michelle wanted to sit me down and have a drink to 'reminisce the old days' as she had so eloquently put it. Translation; 'We want to poke and prod you and see how you're really doing.'

Almost on cue, Michelle placed a hand on my arm and looked sympathetically at me. "I really was sad to hear about your divorce with Janelle. What happened exactly?"

"If you want me to spill everything, you're going to need to get me a bigger glass," I said, holding up the almost empty glass of gin. "In fact, bring the bottle."

"When was the last time you talked to her?"

Pinching the bridge of my nose, I shut my eyes, knowing she wouldn't let it rest. "The day the final divorce papers needed to be signed. I believe her exact words to me were; 'Goodbye, Detective Crane. I hope you find the mystery you really want'."

"You saw her as a mystery?" Michelle voiced while Leon let her take the lead on this one.

"No, I saw love as a mystery, how stupid, really. I now see how simple it is. How useless." I downed the rest of my drink and set it down on the coffee table. Out of the corner of my eye, I saw Michelle frown.

"I sometimes wonder what it must be like to be you," She then said, her voice changing tone. "The infamous Russell Crane, the mastermind and brilliant deductionist. Does it ever get lonely up on that shining pedestal you hoist yourself up on?"

"You were the one who put those labels on me."

"Oh no, I wasn't. We both know given the chance, you'd let the whole world know you're better than the rest of us," Michelle interrupted, crossing her legs. "But at the end of the day, you're still as human as the rest of us, Russell. You were created by the same God that created the—"

"There is no God, stop deceiving yourself."

"No, you stop deceiving yourself," Michelle snapped, sitting up. I turned my head to look at her when her voice raised. "You loved Janelle, Russell, you can explain it however you want, but you shared a real bond with her; a bond you only ever shared with mystery and enigmas before her!"

I pressed my lips into a flat line as Michelle paused to take a breath. Receiving a mouth-lashing was also one of the reasons I abandoned the marital life. Janelle—whenever she had gotten pissed and had given me one herself—usually went on for hours, lecturing me on shit I had no interest in whatsoever. Love, as obsessed as the rest of the world was with it, wasn't my thing. Janelle finally figured that out and left me. Hopefully Michelle and Leon would, too, soon.

"Leaving Janelle left a scar on you." Michelle finally said, sighing. "You're still recovering, all these things you are doing—burying yourself in your work, drinking and doing drugs, sleeping with that neighbor of yours..."

I instantly glared up and turned my eyes to Leon. "Since when did you become a gossip girl, Leon?"

He scoffed and sipped his beer. "I'm worried about you, Russ. You said it yourself, she's a nymphomaniac. I did a little background check on her and—"

"You did what?" I snapped. "You researched Amy?"

Leon slowly smirked and leaned back. "No, but would you look at that; You cared." When I scoffed and rolled my eyes, he chuckled. "Yeah, you're not the only one who can do mind games. Are you falling for this girl?"

I glared coldly at him and clenched my jaw. "No. She was a distraction from the drugs I wanted to take. When the Russians took a swing-by at my apartment, I made it clear to her that we were over. She got it, she understood it could harm her knowing me. As far as I'm concerned, she's out of the picture."

"Mm-hm." Leon sarcastically grunted. "Whatever you say, man. That's your business, we're just here having this conversation because we as your friends worry about you."

"Well that's a complete waste of time."

"Is it?" Michelle now voiced. "Because from where I'm sitting, you're one moment away from breaking down."

"Maybe you need to relocate, then."

"I'm serious," She said, pursing her lips. "Don't isolate yourself, come to us. We want to help you through this."

"Through what, exactly? What's your prognosis, doc?" I sarcastically drawled. "You've been shrinking me for nearly half an hour now, what's the diagnosis? Heartbreak? Trauma? Perhaps insanity?"

"Loneliness," She said. "You're lonely, Russell. You find comfort in mysteries because they can keep your head busy and distracted from the fact that you push people away. You're an individual, we all know that, and you feel left out."

"Jesus Christ, I need that bottle of gin now," I sighed. "Stop it, Michelle, don't bother analyzing me, not unless you want me to return the favor."

"You're are a detective," She stated, folding her arms. "Maybe you should put yourself under the magnifying glass for once and see what you find."

Gnashing my teeth, I abruptly stood up. "You don't get it, do you? I know I have problems, but I just don't care about them. The fact that you've taken on the task of trying to fix me is exhausting, because I don't want fixing," I snarled at Michelle. "I want a goddamn case, I want to sleep with whomever I want without being asked if I'm falling in love, and I want to take the fucking pantothenic acids I use to hype my brain without getting lectured like a rouge teenager by an old married couple who thinks they got the world down, just because they love each other," I turned to Leon who stood up when I clenched my fists. "Tell Michelle about Vegas. Let's see how strong your precious love will be then."

Turning on my heel, I grabbed my jacket and headed for the door. I didn't wait for their reply as I swung it open and walked out, heading for the main road. I hailed the first cab and got in, asking him to take me to my apartment.

I was done hiding. It was time to get back in the game. After all, I had a little girl to find.

I stepped over the threshold to my apartment and looked around. Someone had fixed it. Probably Leon. The furniture had been replaced and repaired—the apartment transformed back into an inhabitable place. My conscience told me to give him a call and thank him, but like always, I blocked that voice out and listened to my own; It told me to go to sleep.

I tiredly walked into my bedroom and looked at the fresh mattress and bedcovers. I let myself fall down into them, resting my head against the headboard and closed my eyes. God, I needed sleep.

"You like that, baby? I know you do. You love my dick."

I opened my eyes again and listened to the sounds coming from the other side of the wall.

"Yeah, baby, oh yeah. I love your tits. Fuck, you feel so great."

Resisting the urge to scoff, I instead started massaging my temples. If that was his idea of bedroom talk, it was pathetic. I could think of so many things wrong with those words, and yet he was still the one fucking Amy.

The grunting noises kept going, but I hardly ever heard her make a sound. The bedsprings creaked, the pace quickened, but I couldn't hear her. Finally, I heard Maddox reach his climax, and with a long moan, the creaking of the bed stopped and was replaced with his short grunts.

"That felt so good, baby. I missed you. Was it good for you, too?"

Was he kidding? What woman wanted a man in the bedroom who had to question if what he did was good for her or not? Either he knew his shit well enough to know that he didn't need to ask, or he should be able to tell whether or not the woman was enjoying it. Obviously, he knew neither.

I heard muffled voices speak for a minute or two, but then they finally stopped. The noises died.

And if I didn't know better, I could have sworn a part of me did, too.

CHAPTER 10

"D o you have any batteries?"

It was déjà vu. We had both been here before, only first time she'd sounded seductive, not suicidal. Her voice wasn't crumbling or hoarse and her attire wasn't this messy; Wrinkled oversized, pinstriped man's dress-shirt and boxers. Not too far from my dirt-stained T and worn-out jeans. We'd make a fine couple in the grunge fashion industry.

She refused to meet my eyes and I knew why. She couldn't stand looking at me, but she was desperate right now. Maybe even humiliated, having to come here and ask me. Her survival technique was to have an orgasm whenever she felt like this, and clearly Maddox hadn't performed admirably last night. A shitty part of me was glad that he didn't. The non-shitty part of me hated seeing her in this condition.

So therefor, I asked, "A+?"

She nodded silently, sniffling. As she lifted her arm to pull a lock of hair behind her ear, I instinctively caught her wrist.

Four small bruises with the same size as fingertips tinted her skin. "Is this what he considers as making love?"

She pulled her arm out of mine and covered it up with her sleeve. "I-I like it that way."

"Sure you do."

"Stop it." She whispered, still not meeting my eyes. "Do you have any batteries or n-not?"

Without further ado, I went up to my smoke alarm in the kitchen, yanked the batteries out and walked back. I handed them to her.

Her cheeks were stained with dried tears and her eyes looked swollen and red, suggesting that she had cried recently and for a long period of time. Her hair was unwashed and uncombed, indication lack of hygiene which probably meant she was depressed. Her skin looked bleaker than normal, paler, indicating she might not have been enjoying the beach as mu--

"Don't."

My eyes traveled up to hers which were now finally staring back at me. They were flickering with pain. "Don't what?"

"I can see it in your eyes and you're making a deduction. Don't."

"Okay." And I meant it. For four whole seconds, I simply stared at her and she stared back.

Then, she dropped the batteries to the floor and jumped me. My arms caught her as our lips clashed, finding each other in need.

Amy moaned and I held her tighter while she grasped my black stained T-shirt and dragged me closer. I kicked the door to my apartment shut, and just like that, we were heading for my bedroom.

She pulled my shirt off on the way, I ripped hers off, buttons flying. My pants were unzipped and yanked down, her boxers went too. In the blink of an eye, I had her down on my bed, kissing my way up her stomach to her breasts.

Amy arched her back and dug her fingers into my messy hair, moaning pleasurably when I bit into her nipple. Blindly, while kissing my way up her décolletage, throat and jaw, I dug my hand into my nightstand, searching for a condom. I found one and pulled back to sheathe myself.

Amy was panting heavily, looking up at me with blazing eyes. I came down on her again and angled myself between her legs, balling them up. In one solid thrust I penetrated her, drawing a loud cry from her. She arched her back again and gripped onto my shoulders as I started moving inside her. Each thrust made her shudder and moan, and each time I felt myself slowly get sober, yet drunker at the same time.

My lips found hers and our tongues mingled. Hot breaths shot out of our mouths, our fingers intwined, our bodies started to glisten with sweat. I hit her centre each time I thrust inside her, and slowly, I could sense her ōrgasm coming. At last, she threw her had back and screamed, coming so hard around me, it released my own climax. I let go with a long groan, jerking inside her as my tip erupted. I filled up the condom and collapsed on top of her, probably suffocating her. But as both of our orgasms subsided and I tried to roll off her, she wrapped her arms around me and kept me put. For just a moment, we laid there, breathing.

Then finally, I drew back a little and looked at her. She met my eyes with her own soft chocolate ones, simply glazing back at me, hers wet with tears. She looked... broken.

You did that to her. You broke her. Nice going, Detective. Your job is to help people, yet you managed to completely break this one. Go put on that Purple Heart medal they gave you. No seriously - go put it on.

I shut my eyes and instead finally rolled off her. She let me, even if it seemed reluctant. I threw an arm over my eyes, not wanting to see her looking the way she did - not wanting to see what I had made her look like.

"When did you get back?" Her voice was barely a whisper.

"Last night."

"Where have you been?"

"You don't want to know."

"Yes I do."

"I was out getting high."

A long pause stretched where she didn't move or speak. Then finally; "Are you high now?"

I sighed and removed my arm. "No."

Her eyes softened and she slowly lifted herself up on her elbow. "Russell, I know what you said two weeks ago wasn't to--"

"Hurt you. I know you do, you're clever enough to understand that where I'm heading is a path that requires no companion."

Another short silence. "How about just company, then?"

I swirled my eyes to meet hers. "Company?"

She nodded and licked her lips. "We don't have to follow the same path, but that doesn't mean they still can't meet once in a while. Like this."

I frowned at her. Was she actually suggesting a fuck-buddy relationship with a drug-addicted detective who was currently on the Russian Mafia's radar of people to mess with? "And here I thought you were smart, Amy."

"What?"

"I don't cross paths with anyone," I snapped and sat up, throwing the covers off. "Actually no, scratch that, I do cross paths with someone; They're called criminals, and as of some time ago, I am officially on all of their hitlists."

"Russell--"

"It was good seeing you again Amy, I hope those batteries still work."

The thick, throbbing silence that felt afterwards was excruciating and I damned myself for letting it reach my heart. When the fuck did this woman get under my skin? She was like a virus to my system. I didn't want it, I didn't need it. Yet I still got it and now it was coursing around in my veins, weakening me. Making me vulnerable.

I had to heal myself, and the only way to do that was to get an antidote; A new drug.

"I'm heading in to work," I said, pulling on my pants before grabbing my dirty shirt. I combed a hand through my tousled hair. "You should head home. Goodbye, Amy."

I couldn't even wait for her reply. I had to get out of there before a repeat of our most recent activity occurred. I was weak. So fucking weak.

"Incredible what a shower and a shave can do to you. You actually look human again."

I ignored Leon's sarcastic voice and buckled my belt. Showering at the police station had been my only option. I couldn't be close to my apartment. And of course Leon had payed notice to that; The one time he actually used his sense of deduction was the one time I wished he wouldn't.

"How did things go back home with Amy and all that? Did you run into her?"

"I found some abandoned locations during my time on the street," I said, ignoring him again. I pulled out the black striped tie and slung it around my neck. "While they to the unobservant audience looked ripped of all their previous values, traces of what happened there were still visible on closer inspection."

Leon seemed to let his own question pass and followed my drift. Thankfully. "So what did you find?"

"Traces of a certain oil only used to maintain a certain kind of boat. Cargo ships. Furthermore, I found fragments of a thick metallic blue paint which under a microscope appeared to be the coating seal of a shipping container. Traces of rust within the sample narrowed it down to a container which has been in use for nearly three years and suffered exposure to sea salt. Finally, I also found microfibers in a small bib which contained cigar smoke particles."

"A bib?"

"This led me to the deduction that our Russian mob has sought out shelter close to the docks, most likely to be closer to their shipment orders. Or perhaps to have a quick get-away."

"Christ. Anything else?"

"I found pollens from a certain flowering plant."

Leon was quiet for a long dead moment. "Don't tell me..."

"Rosæ calyx," I voiced, tightening the tie. "A rosebud. A clue left there on purpose for me since that particular species doesn't grow in this area."

"Shit," Leon cursed. "Russ, what does this mean?"

"It means we are heading down to the pier, comerate," I replied, coating the last word in a thick Russian accent. "A certain Rose is waiting for us."

"And you're sure she's there?"

I just glared at him.

Signing, he picked up the cell in his belt and dialed a number while I pulled down the collar of my green shirt, fixing it.

"This is officer Leon Jones, requesting for a full back-up SWAT team. The Russian Mafia's headquarters have been located and with all due respect, we intend to bring these fuckheads down. Standing by for confirmation."

"All units stand by. Nobody moves until I command otherwise," Leon gruffly spoke into his mic. The SWAT team had surrounded a building I had identified to be the chosen one, especially after seeing the two full-blooded Russians standing guard outside. So far they hadn't spotted anything unusual which was impressive, considering the swarm of policemen that Leon had called for. It was godawful to say the least.

Right now for example, I was crouching behind a large barrier, waiting for... well, for fucking chaos to explode. Their game plan was to storm the building. Nobody bothered to listen to me when I told them that was a horrible idea. Leon just dragged me along instead and kept me for translation.

"Alright, Russ, you're up."

Leon handed the binoculars over to me and I took them with a flat glare. I then zoomed in on the men outside the building by the pier and I squinted my eyes. I watched their lips closely.

"What are they saying?" Leon asked from my left. "Are they speaking Russian or English?"

I watched their mouths chew on their syllables and spit them out like snuff. "Russian."

"Can you tell what they're saying?"

I blinked, concentrating on their lips. It wasn't an easy task lip-reading a Russian from 50 feet away, but it was me.

"Stop messing around with that, asshole. Vahlov said to keep an eye open for the police."

"Those spineless dicks won't have the guts come here," The other man replied, spitting on the ground while keeping a hand on the gun sitting in his belt which was covered by his jacket. "We could rape their fucking wives and they wouldn't face us like real men."

"Do you think the clever blond will come?" The first one asked, lighting up a smoke. That made it so much harder to read his lips.

"I would if I was him," The second guy snorted. "Did you see what they did to his woman? I would be mad as fuck if it was mine."

My brain went into a freeze; Something it had never done before. I wish I could replay his words and read them again, just so I was sure I didn't get it wrong. But I hadn't.

"Yeah, what a mess," The first guy continued. "But she's still alive, right?"

"Only just. After Vlad had his turn with her, I wouldn't count on her pussy still being in one piece. She cried like a baby when Dhargo joined. They took her from the front and back at the same time while they had her chained to the ceiling. They fucked her so hard she passed out from the pain. I gotta give it to her, she could take a proper dicking, even when unconscious. I think they split her pussy in half, though."

It took my absolute everything not to whirl around, grab Leon's gun and fire away. Instead I slowly turned around, handing the binoculars back to Leon.

My blood was boiling, my brain was throbbing and my body was shaking with anger. They had taken Amy. They had raped her because of me. It was my fault they had taken her because I couldn't control myself.

"Russ, answer me, man. What did they say? Have they hurt the girl?"

I took a deep breath, clenching my fists. My brain was working on high pressure right now. More so than usual.

"The girl is fine. It's me they want. They were talking about how Vahlov wants to have a talk with me."

"Shit," Leon cursed, scratching his jaw. "Well then you're staying here. Obviously."

"No, obviously I got to go in," I glared back. "If there's even the slightest chance that Vahlov will listen to me, I could perhaps convince him to hand over the kid peacefully. In any case, I can stall him for a long time by using acrobatically difficult words to speak."

"That is if he doesn't shoot you first," Leon retorted, giving me a dry look. "You're not going in there, Russ. You're a private detective--"

"--who just so happens to speak Russian fluently," I fired back. "There are two ways this can go down; One, either you let me go in there and stall time for you, or two; I go in there myself. It's a free country."

Leon looked at me like I was insane and cursed to the sky, before finally running a hand over his afro. "You are goddamn suicidal, Russell! You go in there, they'll kill you! And not even your brain can talk your way out of that."

"I'll actually take that bet."

"I'm not betting you, I'm telling you. You're not going in there, that's final. Think about Amy."

"I am," I said, gritting my teeth. "I'm sorry Leon, but you give me no choice."

"Oh no, don't even think abou--"

I jumped up over the barrier and ran. Leon didn't get a chance to get a hold on me before I was gone. The last thing I heard was Leon yelling into his mic to stand down and not shoot the maniac running across the grounds. I bolted head first towards the Russian Headquarter, slowing my pace as I got closer. The two guards outside noticed me and immediately drew their weapons. I stopped, holding up my hands. "Easy, I'm just making your job a whole lot simpler. You wanted me, didn't you? Here I am."

The two Russians exchanged a skeptic look before they came closer. One of them pulled out a walkie-talkie and said a codeword. What that codeword meant was obvious, and I really hoped it was to the normal-minded person, too.

"I'm not armed," I said, rolling my eyes as they stalked closer, guns prepared. "There's no need to warn the squad, believe me. I'm not stupid enough to fight."

"Shut up," The first guard said in a very rusty English. "You don't speak."

I rolled my eyes again, pressing my lips together. If they wanted silence, then that's what they got.

"Don't move, hands behind your head," The other one said as he came up to me, patting me down for weapons. I calmly stood while he checked me, obviously coming up short. "He's clean."

The other guard nodded, narrowing his eyes at me. "What is your game, detective?"

"I can speak now?" I flatly asked. "I came by because I believe you have something that doesn't belongs to you."

I noticed the Russians exchange a pointed look before they both smirked sinisterly. Finally, one of them grabbed my hands, twisted them behind my back and locked them with a set of cuffs. "Come with us, Detective."

They led me into the building while I felt Leon's binoculars bore into my back.

Sometimes, actions like these were necessary. And some-times - like now, when I saw the first Russian guy discretely pull out a set of brass knuckles - you first had to endure pain to get what you wanted.

CHAPTER 11

"Detective Russell Crane," Vahlov said in dense Russian. "It's an honor to finally meet you in person."

Wincing in pain as the Russian guard Gustav yanked my head up by my hair, I looked up at mafia boss Vahlov Pretikov, who in all his not-so-mighty-glory came into the room I'd spent my last hour getting more than beaten up in and then some. But I was still conscious, so there was that.

"Beating me up first and then shoving me onto my knees in front of you like a slave?" I dryly said, spitting out a mouthful of blood. "It's so stereotypical. I must confess I had hoped for more."

"I know you speak Russian. You are in my house. Consider yourself unheard until you speak our tongue."

"Well you're in my country. Consider yourself an illegal immigrant until you pass a citizenship test."

To my surprise, Vahlov started laughing. He gave me a amused grin before smoothing down his goatee. "My men call you 'the clever blond'. I am beginning to see why. Do you have a comeback for everything?"

"Never underestimate the power of a decent vocabulary. Where is she?"

"Where is who?" Vahlov theatrically hummed before snapping his fingers. "Oh, you mean your little girlfriend. Don't worry, she's safe where she is. As long as you do what I say, she won't get harmed. Now, please speak my tongue, I find the English language so tiring. And if you want your little girlfriend to stay unharmed..."

"You already harmed her," I replied, coating on a thick Russian. "I heard your guards outside speak - or rather I saw them."

"Ah yes, you read lips," Vahlov chuckled, crossing his arms across his chest. "They say you can find out everything about a person simply by looking at them."

"You're changing the subject on purpose."

"Perhaps I am," Vahlov mused. "But if you want to see your girlfriend, you'll do best to humor me."

With the memory of what the two guards had said about her and what they had done, I gritted my teeth and swallowed my massive pride. "What do you want from me?"

"First I want to see you dance," Vahlov grinned grimly. "I'm sure you know a lot about me already, but what can you tell me about myself from where you're kneeling?"

"You have had a recent injury to your left shin, my guess is a bullet," I flatly replied, purposely switching back to English. "You've recently also started training that leg, but you pulled a muscle, so now you're in constant pain. You're too much of a man to see a doctor or take pills for it, and speaking of things you should be getting treatment for, I've heard syphilis is a bitch. Oh, and you had pelmeni for lunch with a side of garlic bread and vodka. Very Russian, I might add."

Vahlov stiffened at my deduction, sending a glare to the guard keeping me seated on the floor. If I turned my head up now, I was certain I would see Gustav there fighting a grin by the mention of his boss's STD. Vahlov turned an angry red color. "You - stand guard outside. I'll handle this American myself."

Gustav the guard left the room quickly, and I kept on staring arrogantly at Vahlov who was grinding his molars and muttering angry curses in Russian. "How can you possibly know such things? Nobody knows. Nobody."

"Well I'm not a nobody, am I, Vahlov?"

Vahlov grimaced viciously at me. "Explain it."

"Alright, but I'm warning you," I said, pursing my lips a little. "You'll feel like an idiot once I'm done, I guarantee it. An even bigger one, that is. I do intent to enjoy making myself look superior and others a fool, or so I've been told."

"Try me."

I smirked to myself. I really did enjoy this part too much, didn't I? "Let's start with your leg, then. It was obvious from the sound of your footsteps when you came in the door that you were limping. When Gustav pulled my head up, I noticed you favored your right leg rather than your left, probably to ease the pressure you must be feeling whenever you support your weight on your bad leg. Now how did I know it was a bullet? Well in your line of business, a bullet is much more likely than a stab wound, and besides, who the hell stabs someone on their shin? Balance of probability. Next, the working out; You obviously didn't seek medical attention when after you got shot, so you decided to train it yourself. My guess is that you probably tore a muscle when you didn't give it enough time to heal properly, and then the training probably snapped it completely.

"What's next, the syphilis? Oh yeah, you've scratched your groin so many times, it has now left a particular scratch pattern on your suit - not noticeable unless you're me of course, so don't worry unless Gustav narks you out, your secret is safe. So how come I knew it was syphilis? Again, balance of probability, it's the most common STD, and frankly just too many prostitutes have it today, you might want to reconsider your taste in women, though given why we are gathered here today, I'd say you've long ago given up on changing style.

"Lastly your lunch," I said, glaring coldly up at Vahlov, when all he was stare back at me with an ominous face. "Pelmeni has a very distinct smell, yet was almost masked by the garlic. Garlic is not a usual ingredient in the pelmini dumplings and you had a tiny bread crumb on your shirt. Ergo, I must assume the garlic came from the bread. And as for the vodka? It was just so goddamn Russian, I threw it in there for good measure, now are we done here, or would you like me to deduce you even further, because I could do this all fucking day."

Vahlov looked at me for another long moment before he broke out into a wide grin. "Impressive! Very impressive, detective Crane, I must say. You have keen eye for details."

"And you have a knack for getting on the lesser side of the law," I replied, straightening out. "Enough with the games, Vahlov. Where is she?"

"I told you, she is safe where she--"

"I'm talking about Rose," I snapped. "The kid. Where is she?"

Vahlov slowly smirked and then took a seat in a chair by a long table. He smoothed over his goatee again before he spoke, "You know... any other man wouldn't have caught that piece of information, Detective. Her name. I quite like it, I must confess. It provided me with the perfect metaphor."

"Now provide me with an actual answer. Where. Is. She?" I growled.

Vahlov chuckled to himself. "You know, Detective, there is one thing I have yet to ask you. It is something that has been bothering me; Why did you take interest in my case? A lost kid and a dead prostitute seems a little too trivial for a smart detective like yourself."

"Exactly. It was too trivial, but not for me. For you," I replied. "We both knew you lured me in, Vahlov. I've played along so the dumbfuck cops outside wouldn't suspect any-thing, but you orchestrated this case for me. You wanted me to come to you, so here I fucking am. What do you want from me?"

"It is not what I want from you, it is what I want to do to you," Vahlov said, his voice now darkening. "Two years ago, Moscow. You were following a case that led you to Russia. Remember who you were investigating?"

"So that's your vendetta?" I scoffed. "Revenge for taking down your brother's cartel and ensuring him the death penalty?"

"You killed my brother!" Vahlov roared and slammed a steel fist into the wooden table. "You took my only family from me, or so I thought until I found Rose. She was my opportunity, and when I heard you had permanently moved to Miami, I saw another one. I could take two birds with one stone, oh but not before messing with you."

"So you took the neighbor I've been casually fucking? That's the best you can do?"

"You and I both know she is more than casual to you," Vahlov smirked and pointed at me. "You hide love well on your face, Detective, but I know when a man is, ah... what is the American expression... whipped."

I gritted my teeth. Sonofabitch. "Whipped or not, you think you'll be able to get to her through me?"

"I have no intentions of getting to you through her," Vahlov chuckled and stood up. "I prefer a more... direct approach."

The door to the room then suddenly opened and three guards walked in. Two of them went up to me and grabbed me firmly, the last one came up to Vahlov and handed him a box, then retrieved to a corner and stood by.

I didn't bother struggling the two guards seen as though it was pointless. I had to preserve energy, and after the beating Gustav administered on me, I wasn't as high in stock as I'd hoped I would be.

Vahlov now opened the box and pulled out a syringe. The fluid inside was honey colored. "You know, I am surprised how far technology has come today. In my days, we didn't have medicine like this," Vahlov said and held up the needle. "My mother gave me vodka whenever I was feeling sick and it knocked me right out. This, however..." He said, coming closer with the needle. "Well, this won't knock you out."

I actually begun wrestling in the guards hold now. I didn't know what that shit was, but I knew I didn't want it near me, much less inside me.

Vahlov came up to and grabbed my hair by the roots and yanked my head up. I glared coldly up at his black eyes, watching how they darkened even more. "This is for my brother."

"No, don't - don't!" I yelled as he yanked my head to the side and thrust the needle deep into my neck. He squeezed the syringe and I groaned as the drug poured into my body and begun working.

I was officially fucked.

CHAPTER 12

I breathed in strongly through my nose as the metal door behind me got shut and locked, incarcerating me in whatever windowless cell this was. One hard white lamp shun from above and made my head hurt and my retinas burn as the drugs in my system throbbed through my veins.

I groaned and rolled over on the floor, squeezing my eyes shut as I felt my skin get bathed in the sweat my body was producing as a way of trying to excrete the poison from my system. My head pulsed like one big artery, feeling like it was swelling up inside my head. A high-pitched whistling sound kept ringing in my ears, along with the heavy throb in my temples.

I didn't know what the drug was or what it did, I didn't even know if it was fatal. All I knew was that my head was overwhelmed by the drug and that whatever it was, it was meant to torment me.

I rolled over on my hands and knees and tried to stop my brain from overcooking. I needed to gain control, I needed to focus...

"Ru... Russell..."

I opened my eyes and immediately swung my head to the thin mattress I hadn't noticed yet. It was shoved up against one of the walls. On top of it was... Amy.

"Russell..." Her voice was barely a hoarse whisper. She was naked, lying on her stomach, her skin bruised and her face beaten. She looked at me with weak eyes.

"Amy... No..."

"Y-you pushed me away..." She whispered, her eyes and skin so pale and lifeless. "You pushed me away to... protect me..."

"Amy, I'm so sorry..."

"They took me..." She closed her eyes, perhaps too tired to keep them open. "They took me a-and they raped me a-and its your fault..."

"Amy, please forgive me, I--"

"You shouldn't have slept with me. You could've kept me safe. This is all your fault. Because of you, they harmed me. Because of you... I'm dying."

"Amy!" I hastily crawled up to the pallet, collapsing when I got to it. The throb in my head was getting worse, pounding me. I reached out to her. "Amy, I'm so sorry..."

She disappeared. I looked down at the pallet. She wasn't there.

"Russell..."

I whipped around and now saw Amy being pressed up against the wall by Gustav. I hadn't heard him come in. He had his hand locked around her throat and his hips pushed against hers. She was still naked.

"You did this to me." She said, looking at me as Gustav begun taking roughly and forcefully up against the wall, her face staying as lifeless as ever. "You didn't protect me."

"No!" I roared and leaped for Gustav, fully intent on killing him with my bare hands, even though I wasn't in my right mind. But as I grasped for him, I collided with the wall, falling back against the floor with a heavy thump. She was gone again. They both were.

It was the drug. It was hallucinogenic. It was making me see things, it was twisting my reality.

"Russell..."

"No!" I said, rolling over onto my knees. I covered my ears and squeezed my eyes shut. "You're not there, you're not real..."

"You're shutting me out again... that's how I ended up her e... you weren't there to protect me..."

"I was trying to protect you by making you stay away!" I roared, vigorously shaking my head. I needed to stop listening, I had to block everything out...

"But you didn't stay away... you came back because you were too weak... too weak to keep me safe..."

"I... I didn't come back for you..."

"Yes, you did. You missed me and when you heard me with Maddox, it hurt you. So when I came to you the next morning, you wanted to get me back and show me how love should really be. But instead you sacrificed my safety... for love. You are weak, Russell."

I was weak. I knew what love could do to a person, yet I had still let it happen. I had let myself lose control and that had resulted in Amy being...

I squeezed my eyes even more shut and suppressed a cry. God, what had I done...

"Why didn't you protect me, Russell? You thought leaving me alone was the safest thing for me?"

"I thought... I thought maybe Leon had put surveillance on you..." I whispered, sinking my head. "That after the break-in, he'd keep you monitored..."

"You think I'd help you after what you did to me?"

I whipped around and saw Leon leaned up against the wall. He looked miserable. His police badge was bended and almost broken, his name nearly scratched off. His attire was wrinkly and stained, his shirt unbuttoned and hanging loosely, not tugged into his pants. His brown skin looked graying, his chin was unshaven. His short afro was untamed and his eyes were bloodshot and hollow. He held a cheep bottle of whiskey in his hand and he was barely standing on his feet.

"Leon..."

"You betrayed me," He said, glaring down at me with hurt in his eyes. "I trusted you. You told my wife about Vegas. You knew it was an accident, I was drunk. That woman kissed me and I was too drunk to stop it! You told Michelle and she left me... you ruined my marriage."

I gripped on to the roots of my hair and forced myself to look away. "It's not real, irs not real, it's not real..." Leon and Michelle were still together... my revelation hadn't hurt their marriage... I hadn't ruined them...

"I was your only friend, Russ. I was the only one who gave you a shot. I put up with your temper, I had your back and you betrayed me. Now Michelle is gone, she took my kids... Lea, Sara, JJ... gone. Some friend you are. I even stood by you through your divorce with Janelle, and now you're can't be there for me because you were the one who ruined my life..."

I roared and squeezed my head, shaking it even more. "Stop it!"

Suddenly there was rustling outside the door. I heard the lock go, and when I faintly looked up, I saw Vahlov standing there. He was smirking grimly at me. "Enjoying your meds, Detective?"

I just hissed at him and squeezed my eyes shut. I had dealt with stronger drugs than this one, I could pull through this one, too.

"Well, in any case, we thought you might like some company. It's an old friend of yours, it's been a few years, but I'm sure you still remember her."

Her?

I looked up as a guard showed up in the frame of the door, and then he pushed inside a woman. She stumbled inside with her hands locked behind her back and then the door was locked firmly again.

I stared, mortified. "Janelle?"

My ex-wife looked at me with her strong amber eyes through her brown lashes. "Did you finally find the mystery you were looking for?"

I shook my head. No... Not her, not Janelle. She couldn't be here, how could they have--

"Do you love her more than you loved me? Do you think sleeping with her will mend the damage you inflicted upon yourself, by screwing things up with me?"

It was the drug again. She wasn't really here, she was just a hallucination.

I turned away and roared into the cell, the vibration of my voice booming against the concrete walls and floors. I squeezed my hands over my ears again, trying to block out the voices. The only problem was, the voices were in my head.

"You loved me, Russell and I loved you. So much. But you couldn't even leave your work long enough to commit. You nearly died, remember? Because you couldn't stop. Your assignment, two years ago; The military contacted you personally because of the national threat..."

"Stop it... don't talk about it..."

"A terror threat was made, the daughter of a high-standing person was captured and used as a bargaining ship; Hand over the commanding chief in charge of protecting military secrets, or she died."

"Don't, please... don't bring it up..."

"You were supposed to figure out where she was being held captive, based on the video they sent, and you did. You found the place and you found the girl..."

"Stop it!"

"How old was she, Russell? Seven? Eight? What would she have been today?"

"STOP!" I roared, hyperventilating. "I know I screwed up! I KNOW!"

"You ignored their threats about how they would kill her if anyone but the commanding chief turned himself over at the mentioned location. But you couldn't resist, could you? You went in his place so you could show how magnificent you were, so you could brag to them about your brilliant deductions that led you to their actual location - the location that the military was about to storm."

I felt my head throb heavier and heavier for each word my ex-wife spoke. Her voice was as clear as crystal.

"You thought your little stunt would distract them. That making them think they were getting the commanding chief would make them forget about watching the little girl. But they didn't. They killed that little girl because you were there. And remind me, how did they kill her again?"

"Don't... I'm so s-sorry..."

"A bomb. They blew her up into pieces. Her parents buried an empty casket because there weren't even as much as two adjoining limbs, but the military still put an honorary Purple Heart on you for finding the terrorists hideout and helping them defeat a national threat. The commanding chief and the military secrets were safe, but that little girl died."

My eyes were burning with tears I didn't even know I had the ability or heart to produce anymore, but then again... I didn't know who I was anymore.

"You tell yourself each day; 'people die,'" My ex-wife's voice coldly continued inside my head, "But that day... she didn't die. You killed her. You wear her blood on your hands each day and no amount of drugs or alcohol will make you forget that. Now you're trying make up for what you did that day by rescuing this little girl. You think you'll succeed in that? How is it going so far, Detective?"

I couldn't listen to it anymore. The drug was overpowering my brain, but one percent was still mine to control. And that was all I needed.

I stuck two fingers down my throat and retched everything I had inside me out onto the floor. I went once, twice, thrice. Then I gurgled some smaller ones up. Eventually, I could feel the throb in my head lighten, even if only a little. What I really needed was a splash of cold water and an IV drip, but I doubted Vahlov took any prison requests. I had to make due with simply throwing up as much as the drug as I could and it actually helped a little.

I then crawled over to the mattress and nestled myself on my left side in the classic recovery position which allowed my breathing to get better. I then rested, chanting the same thing over and over in my head again, until I drowned out all the other voices. It was a poem by Gerard Nolst Trenité called The Chaos. I had memorized it for situations like these where I couldn't control my brain. It was the perfect distraction and it gave me time to figure out my next move.

"Wakey, wakey, Detective. Are you ready to talk some more?"

I opened my eyes to the sound of the Russian words and was instantly wide away. The drug has left my system, my head was clear. I was ready.

Vahlov's dogs pulled me to my feet and clamped a pair of handcuffs around my wrists behind my back, then led me out of the prison cell, down a couple corridors. My mind had never been more awake, more lucid. Finally they pushed me into the same room as earlier, and just like earlier, they shoved me to my knees in front of a chair where Vahlov was sitting comfortably.

"Detective," Vahlov greeted me in flat Russian, of course. "How are you feeling? Did you enjoy your medication?"

"As a matter of fact I did," I replied back in smooth English. "It was quite helpful, I must say."

"Helpful?" Vahlov questioned and lifted a brow. "How so?"

"It made me realize how stupid I've been."

"Oh?"

"I've been blind," I said, meeting Vahlov's eyes. "The evidence was right there in front of me and I never saw it. But now I do."

"What was?" Vahlov's unconsciously switched to English and his voice was getting angrier. I also noticed his nostrils flared. He didn't like not being in the know.

"All the signs where there, I can't believe I was so narrow -sighted..."

"Tell me what it is you think you have discovered or be dosed up with another shot!" Vahlov growled furiously, slamming his hand into the table.

"By all means, please do, that's how I figured it out," I said, looking at him. "You are well aware I'm an ex-drug addict, otherwise you wouldn't have chosen drugs as your method of torture. You have more than enough men at your disposal to give me a hard, long suffering death, but giving me drugs would be much, much more satisfying, wouldn't it? To see me crave the next shot, have me begging at your feet for the next fix..."

"Get to your point." Vahlov sneered. He was grinding his molars, but signs of perspiration around his temples showed he feared what I had discovered. And he should. It would be his downfall.

"Well, by being an ex-drug addict, you then must know that I had a far different relationship with drugs than other people," I said, tilting my head to one side. "I don't use them for the rush - or well, I do - but that's only part of it. I find my head gets clearer whenever I use drugs to help with my cases. The only sad thing is you get addicted eventually, so I stopped, but I digress. The thing is," I said, taking a breath "The hallucinogenic drug you gave me isn't an addictive one. It's just a drug that's designed to mess with your head and bring out your demons."

"Last warning, Detective."

"But you failed to realize - and don't feel bad about it, it took me some time to realize, too - that I could also discover your demons, Vahlov."

Vahlov leaned back in his chair and watched me with dark eyes. He didn't say anything, just kept glaring. I took it as a sign to continue.

"The thing about drugs is that when you've tried a lot of them, they all blur together as one. I learned to use drugs in my past to help me see things clearer, and today, once I started seeing the ghosts from my past and they started talking to me, I realized they were also bringing up some things I had been trying to suppress. In other words; They helped me realize a few things I never thought I would."

"So you managed to 'shrink' yourself by talking to manifestations your brain concocted while on a powerful hallucinogenic drug?" Vahlov now countered with a dry scoff. "Maybe that drug was too powerful, after all. You sound mad, Detective."

"On the contrary, it gave me just what I needed," I said, dragging a smirk to my lips. "I've always believed that my own company was the best, and as of today, I've proved it. For while talking to my ghosts, ergo myself, I came upon a discovery. Your drug helped me win this war between us, so I should thank you, Vahlov. You gave me the last aid I needed to see things clearer. I was sober and you gave me a fix."

"This has gone on for long enough." Vahlov snarled. "Either spit it out or find yourself burning in the flames of hell!"

"In that case, I suppose I'll see you soon," I smirked. "For you, Vahlov, are terminally ill."

Chapter 13

"It's not the first time I've made a speedy conclusion," I said, wetting my lips when Vahlov stood up threateningly. "I've actually done that quite a lot lately. I'm ashamed of myself, but then you come along and decide to give my brain a boost. I really do thank you."

"I am not terminally ill," Vahlov sneered in English, probably in hopes that his Russian comrades wouldn't understand.

"But you are. All the signs are there," I said, tilting my head to the side. "Wouldn't you say it's odd for a big-time mafia lord like yourself to not be in charge of doing all the brutal beating? You carry a seriously grudge for me and you obviously like getting your hands dirty if we go by your line of work."

"You little--"

"And don't you think it's odd that a seemingly intelligent man like yourself who can come up with clever metaphors is still stupid enough to refuse medical aid when his leg is clearly in need of it?" I wondered rhetorically. "Unless of course there's something you wouldn't want a doctor to discover by a simple examination. Something like... cancer?"

Vahlov's eyes glinted with wrath. He didn't speak, just stared at me with the promise of a long sufferable death.

Well, if I was going to die, I might as well get my last words out. "Death is an expected but unfortunate part of life, yet when it comes before the senior age, it's considered a sign of weakness. You no doubt hid it from all within your little 'corporation' here, because nothing like illness makes people look at you with pity." I spoke from experience. "If your men knew you were dying or your enemies for that matter, your metaphorical throne would be theirs to easily take. My guess is that you wanted to ensure your noble linage to continue to sit on the throne before you died, so you made sure you had an heir. Sure, a girl might not have been the best option, but given the circumstances she would have to do. Am I getting close?"

Vahlov still didn't speak. I took it as a sign to continue.

"Then of course, all you had to do was capture the one person who could stand in the way of your plan succeeding. The one person who would eventually figure it out and bring you down," I said, meeting his eyes with a little smirk. "Me."

Vahlov's eyes glinted again but this time not from anger, but from excitement. He took two steps closer to me and then shoved his hands into his pants. "Very good, Detective. You should feel proud of yourself."

"I do, continue."

"But aren't you forgetting one thing?" He said and cocked a brow, growing a sly smirk on his lips. "Why do you think that it is that your precious police force haven't stormed this place yet? We know they are out there, waiting."

My mind crunched the various answers, but alas, I came up lacking. I hated that. For once, he had an answer that I didn't. "Alright, I'll bite, Vahlov. Tell me; Humiliate me if you must, my ego can handle it."

"I wouldn't be so sure," He chuckled. "How did you put it..? Ah yes; Don't you think it's odd," he said, mimicking me, "That I haven't put you and your little woman in the same room yet? That I haven't showed you what I've done to her? It must have crossed your mind by now. 'What has he done to her, is she still alive, where is she?'" Vahlov mused. "To answer your question; She's at home. We never took her from you. I told my men to speak offensively about your woman and I guess their imagination ran away with them. But truth be said, detective Crane, she is home in her happy little apartment, doing happy little things, while being happily unaware of your heroic gesture for her," He smirked. "You gave yourself up for nothing."

I closed my eyes and cursed silently in my head when Vahlov began chuckling maliciously. I should have known. No, I should've checked first. Should've called her, heard her voice. I didn't. I blindly took their crass words as truthful and went charging into the battlefield for her.

Fuck, I really was whipped, wasn't I?

"So you see, Detective, the only reason why they haven't stormed this place yet, is because I have threatened to kill you," He told, smirking. "You practically volunteered as a hostage and for that I must thank you."

Sonofabitch. I clenched my fists in rage and sneered at the floor. Vahlov had not only taken care of the only obstacle in his way, being me, he had also lured me into a trap which now held the police from storming this place and saving an innocent little girl. Leon cared too much about me to let my life go that easily and the damned Purple Heart they pinned on me probably kept some of the higher-ranked people from taking command and gunning this place down themselves. They were in a pickle.

"So let me guess," I snarled. "They pay you a handsome fee for me, maybe grant you passage out of the country somehow, in the agreement of getting me back when all is said and done?" I scoffed. "If that's the case, it won't hold. I'm not worth that much to them."

"True, but then again, aren't you?" Vahlov mused. "I know all about you, Detective Crane. I knew you worked for the military a few years back. You were involved in a few classified state secrets." Vahlov walked all the way up to me and leaned down to my face. "How much do you think that information is worth to them? You think they'll take the risk of you spilling it under a torture session?"

"I'll never rat."

"Probably not, but the government doesn't take risks," Vahlov scoffed and stood up. "All the cards are on the table, Detective. Each moment they spend arguing over what to do is a moment where I hypothetically could be extracting you for information. I don't think it will be long before I have what I want," He chuckled, glaring down at me.

I ground my molars. He really had it all figured out. All except one major flaw in his plan. Well, maybe not so major, considering I only just made up my mind. "You say you know everything about me..."

"I do, Detective. I was quite thorough in my investigation of you."

"Well then you must also know that I am an excellent lock-pick." With that, I yanked off the cuffs I had been silently working on picking ever since Gustav dumped me in here. The bed in the excluded cell had a loose spring and guess what? Springs made excellent lock-picks.

I jumped up before Vahlov had a chance to react and throttled my skull into his. Punching him across his jaw and kicking his gut with my knee, he fell to the ground with a groan and a thump. There was no fight at all. Vahlov was weaker than he let on, weakened by his terminal disease. The infected gunshot wound and syphilis was just adding misery to more misery.

I grabbed the Glock from his belt and checked the clip before arming it. Stalking up to the door, I knew I now only had one mission; Find the little girl, get out and let the Feds do the rest. But I wasn't leaving without that girl.

I made sure to handcuff and gag Vahlov properly with the same cuffs he used on me and with the handkerchief in his breast pocket. After that, I knew I'd have to shoot my way out. With no armor or Kevlar, I was most likely to get shot myself. But as long as I could make it to the little girl, I would take as many bullets as my body could swallow.

I'd only ever been shot five times in my whole life; Once in my my shoulder, once in my back, once in my arm and once side in my side and my leg.

- All of them were today.

As I strapped in another clip that I had taken from one of the dead guard's belts, I fired it at the struggling guard on the floor across from me. He had been crawling for his gun, but now... well, the only place he'd be crawling to now was Hell if there even was such a place.

I groaned on the floor and clutched the wound in my side, deciding that that was the one that bled the most. It was the wound in my back that hurt the most, though, but I couldn't quite reach that.

Forcing myself to get up, I stumbled further down the hall, supporting most of my weight by leaning against the wall. One hand on my wound and one hand holding the gun, I let my unwounded shoulder be my wall-support as I soldiered on. Just a few more steps and I'd be at the end of the guarded hallway I had gunned down. Don't ask me how.

Finally standing in front of the locked door, I shot the padlock off and then opened it. What met me was a tiny little girl sitting on a soiled mattress. Pee, from what I could tell and smell. She was clutching on to her teddybear, a bunny plushie of some sort. Her black hair was tousled and looked uncombed, just like the rest of her stained attire did. What the hell had they been doing with this girl? Hadn't the whole idea been to take care of her?

"Hello sweetheart," I said, trying to force as much softness into my voice as possible. Truth was, getting shot hurt, but moving around with open bleeding wounds with bullets inside you hurt more. Soft was a voice that took a lot to muster when you felt like collapsing on the floor from pain. "My name is Russell. I'm from the police. I'm here to help you."

She just begun sobbing, her cries growing louder. That wasn't good.

"Shh, darling," I whispered, kneeling down to her. I carefully picked her up, stroked her hair and placed a kiss on top of her head. "It's okay. Don't be scared. We're going to get you out of here, yeah? Don't worry."

I was speaking to a five-year-old. Telling her not to worry was about as productive, as telling a rock not to sink in water. She kept on crying, but nonetheless found some comfort with me. When I felt comfortable with her trusting me enough to remove her from the environment, I stepped out of the room and begun my march back down the hall.

Step. Pain. Step. Pain. Step.

Her legs were curled around my waist, her right knee digging into the gunshot wound on my right side. Her arms were cinched around my neck, the weight of her head against my shoulder pressing on the wound located there. So much pain. Too much blood lost.

I groaned and nearly collapsed to my knees. Just a little further.

I finally spotted the same door I'd walked in through. The same that would lead me out. I sped up the pace, groaning as the wound in my leg spiked up and made me clench my jaw so hard I swore I cracked a tooth.

A gunshot went off behind me and the next thing I felt was a blinding pain that went through my back to my stomach. I let out a holler and collapsed onto my knees, clutching the little girl. She screamed and clutched me, too. I wouldn't make it. But she could.

"Rose," I whispered, hearing rustling behind me. My deductive senses told me there was one guard I had failed to kill and he was now coming for me, but slowly. He was wounded like me. "Rose, I need you to listen to me; I need you to run out that door and keep running, okay? Ask for someone named Leon. No one else, okay? He's dark, has a big funny nose and there's a small ketchup stain shaped like a heart on his tie. Can you find him for me? Tell him he can come in here now and clean this place up?"

Rose was scared to her tiny bones, but she still nodded. Letting her go, she got to the floor and begun running towards the door with shaky legs, still clutching her teddy. She made it out the door and kept running.

Another gunshot went off, and this time I didn't feel it hit. Then again, I'd lost so much blood, my limbs were going numb.

I fell onto the floor, my chin hitting the dirty concrete. My eyelids slid close on their own accord which saved me or anyone else who found me the trouble of doing it. Opened-eyed corpses were the least attractive ones if you asked me. The least I could do was close my eyes for Leon's benefit, especially since I brought up Vegas to his wife.

I faintly heard footsteps, but they were too far away. The world darkened and I couldn't wait to see what mysteries lied ahead.

After all, I was about figure out the biggest mystery known to mankind; What came next after the darkness?

CHAPTER 14

❝ ..ost a lot of blood. The bullet wound on his side pierced through a part of his intestines which we had to repair. Also the wound on his shoulder fractured his clavicle bone. It's going to take a while to heal. As for the gunshot to his leg, luckily the bullet missed any bones, but it did however tear a muscle. Recovery will take some time, but with the right rehabilitation, he should he alright. No longterm injuries."

"Thank you, Doctor. Oh, one more thing, Miss."

"Yes, Sir?"

"When do you think he'll wake up?"

"We have him under heavy medication, it might take him some time before he--"

"Wakes up?" I hoarsely groaned. My tongue felt like burlap. "Yeah, I've dealt with harder drugs."

"Russ!" Leon walked up to my hospital bed, as did the doctor, both looking stunned. "You goddamn fool. Why don't you ever do as you're told?"

"By now you should know why."

"Yeah? Well maybe getting shot is what you needed then," He scoffed, crossing his arms while the doc checked up on my vitals.

My body felt like tender meat. Maybe I now finally knew how fish felt when they got a hook through their mouth - only the hook was I don't know how many bullets and the mouth was my whole body.

- If that was the case, I just became a vegetarian.

But surprisingly enough, what hurt the most was my head. And damn it if I knew why. "Hey, doc? Mind pulling out that morphine drip? It's not good for an ex-addict to get high."

"I'm sorry Sir, but if we turn of the drip--"

"I'll be in a shitload of pain, but I'd rather be that than go to one more stupid AA meeting. Turn it off."

"Just do as he says," Leon sighed apologetically to the doctor. She gave me a prudent look, but then turned off the morphine drip. Thank the fucking God. There were better things than morphine to get high on. Morphine just made me nauseous.

"So, Russ--"

"I'm sorry about Michelle."

"What?"

"I'm sorry I brought up Vegas to Michelle," I elaborated and tried to wet my dry lips. Didn't work, my tongue still felt like a starfish's arm, all thick and raw.

"I wasn't questioning the Michelle part, I was questioning the sorry bit," Leon replied with a flat look. "I don't think I've ever heard those words come out of your mouth before."

"Well I--"

"Open wide please for a moment." The doctor opened my mouth for me and stuffed a popsicle stick down my throat. I coughed and jerked away from her.

"Jesus woman, do you mind? My tonsils are fine, my pupils respond properly, my only problem is you," I snapped, ignoring the offended glare she gave me. "Go help someone else, I'm sure there are plenty of people in this hospital who needs your popsicles more than me."

"Thank God, I thought for a minute there the Russ I knew had been brain damaged," Leon scoffed while the doctor took my chart and then left, looking like I cursed her children to Hell. "But now you sound like yourself again."

I snorted, which turned out to be a painful act. "You know I don't change, Leon."

"No, you never do, do you?"

I closed my eyes and let out a long breath. "How is Michelle? Is she--"

"She already knew you dipshit."

My eyes flew open again. "What?"

Leon smiled tightly at me. "I told her the same night we came home from Vegas. She wasn't too mad, but she's known for months. You didn't ruin us."

My eyes fell shut again and I exhaled I breath that felt like I just let go of a huge burden. Guilt? "How's the girl? She safe?"

Leon didn't mind my rapid subject change. He knew I was no good with feelings. "She's safe, thanks to you. She came running out and crying my name. I'm guessing you told her to come look for me," He noted whereafter I tiredly nodded. "Then once her safety was ensured, the SWAT teamed moved in and took over. We found you painting the concrete red in the hallway while Vahlov was chained up like a dog with his mouth gagged. Also you, I'm presuming." I didn't bother nodding this time as Leon continued. "Then it was just a matter of rounding up as many of the men you had graciously left alive for us, and take them into custody. Some of them talked and told us what went down, what the whole plan had been." Leon paused and raised a brow at me. "All of this for a woman, Russ. Jesus."

I closed my eyes and cursed silently in my head. Fucking great. Now he was going to bash me on that.

"Speaking of which, she's here."

My eyes flew open. He didn't bash at all. Maybe he was saving it for later when my cheeks were nice and pink again and my scrapes were less obvious. Then he'd attack me for sure, I was positive.

But Amy was here. Alive and well, I assumed. Not harmed, not even a little. No danger around her.

"She's been asking if she can see you."

"Only family is allowed to visit," I curtly replied back. I didn't feel like talking to her about all this. From the look on Leon's face, he had probably told her all about everything. I could deal without having her cooing over how I had 'fallen in love with her'. Dear lord.

"Exactly," Leon replied and straightened out. "Good thing she is your fiancée, then."

"She's what?"

I heard rustling outside the door before a doctor and Amy then stepped through to my room. Leon leaned down to my ear in than moment and whispered quietly, "Play along or she'll get kicked out." When I gave him a flat look that told him I wasn't going to do that, he padded my bad shoulder with a smirk. "That's the least you can do for betraying me on Vegas."

"But she knew, then it's not--" I growled as he walked out, still grinning. He nodded at Amy in the passing who smiled back and then looked at me. Her face instantly paled by the look of my no-doubt gruesome-looking condition.

"It's not as bad as it looks," I told, rolling my eyes. "You can stop looking at me like I'm goddamn dying and start spilling what it is you want to say."

Her face warmed up again, clearly by how I hadn't lost my dry sense of humor. She pulled on a big exaggerated sweet smile and walked up to me. "Oh, honey. I'm so glad you're safe. How are you feeling?"

"Engaged, apparently."

She chuckled heartfully - also fake - and leaned down and pecked a kiss on my forehead. "You silly man, I can't believe I agreed to marry you. Nurse, would you mind if we had a moment alone, please?"

"Of course. I'll be right outside if you need anything," The nurse smiled at our 'loving reunion' and then left us be in my room. Leon had hooked me up with a private one, the asshole. Who the hell was I going to annoy the shit out of now?

"So, honey," I sarcastically scoffed to her delight. "What are you doing here?"

"Just checking up my plaything. Had to make sure it wasn't broken."

I snorted but secretly felt like smiling. I knew there was a reason my idiotic brain decided it liked her pheromones. "I'll be fine in a few weeks. You'll have to do most of the work in the meantime, but I have a feeling it won't be a problem."

"Shouldn't be, no. I purchased these gorgeous new police handcuffs that I just can't wait to try out. And since you won't be able to put up a fight..."

"Very funny. Cut the crap, you know, don't you?"

"Know what?" She smirked innocently, brushing a thumb over my brow, following a suture. "That the carpet matches the drapes? Yes, I do."

"You're going to force me to say it, aren't you?"

"If I can, yes."

"Well you can't, words so stupid will never leave my mouth ever again, they don't mean anything anyway. Chemistry and attraction is shown through touch and bodily intimacy, not through meaningless, corny words that's become a token of great--"

"Oh just fucking say you love me."

"Fine. I love you. Happy?"

She didn't speak, just split her mouth into a wide smile. She then leaned down and pressed a kiss to my lips, a kiss I only partially welcomed and didn't return. She wasn't going to turn all sappy on me now, wasn't she? Good God, what had I gotten myself into again? Wasn't the first time enough? Had I learned nothing?

"Don't get that look now," She said, pulling back and smirking mischievously. "I see that pretty little brain of yours working in overdrive, it's not good for it. Not right now anyway, right now you need to rest. When you get back to your apartment, I'll make sure there'll be something interesting for you to... deduce."

I pursed my lips and looked her up and down. "What are you, Amy? I can never figure you out."

She just smiled and hiked up in her thin bag before walking up to the door. "I'm a woman."

- And that sentence in itself was a mystery.

CHAPTER 15

"You need anymore help?"

"I didn't need help to begin with, so no."

"The doc told you not to walk on that leg."

"She also prescribed me strong meds to keep the pain down - me, an ex-addict. That shows the intelligence levels on that one."

"Russ." Leon set down my bag of clean clothes - a bag of clean clothes that Michelle had washed for me while I was recovering in the hospital - on the floor next to the door and looked at me as I limped to my couch. "Will you be okay by yourself here?"

"We both know I won't be alone. I heard you talking to Amy outside my room in the hospital as I was getting changed. You two are conspiring against me. I believe your exact words were 'check up on him every now and then and make sure he eats--'"

"Alright!" Leon barked. "Just look out for yourself, yeah? I know how you get, you can't sit the goddamn down and relax like the doc told you to."

"Of course I can't. Now that this case is closed, I gotta find a new one. Unless you want me to start taking those pills the doc gave me--"

"The case might be closed but there's still a lot to be done," Leon replied and watched as I started sifting through all the case files, gathering them in an orderly chaos. "Vahlov still needs to face trial, you might have to take the stand, you know. I'm still pissed you didn't tell me he had an agenda towards you."

"What about the little girl? Rose?" I asked, wincing as I accidentally stretched the wound on my back by leaning forward. Ow.

"She's under Child Protective Service. She'll go into a good foster home, get the right counseling. Hopefully she won't have any longterm traumas."

"Good."

A long silence stretched. I was still gathering the files, using one hand since my shoulder and arm was wrapped up in a sling. I could sense that Leon wanted to say something but he was hesitating for some reason.

"Spit it out, will you? If not, then go make oxygen into carbon dioxide out in the hall. You're annoying me."

"You're in love with her, aren't you?" He then said. When I closed my eyes and gritted my teeth, he continued, "You don't have to say, I can tell, Russ. You're crazy about this girl."

"I take it back, don't spit it out, swallow it. Gag on it. Now please leave, I have things to do."

"What is it about her, if I may ask?" Leon continued, ignoring my request for him to go. "I only talked to her a little out in the hall in the hospital, she seemed nice, but that's all I can say. I'm assuming you've spent more time with her, so tell me, what makes her special to you?"

I opened my eyes again and stared straight ahead at the wall. "The same thing that makes Michelle special to you."

When I stood up, wincing as I did, Leon just looked at me with a small frown. I limped to my bedroom, but stopped up in the door. I looked down at my feet.

"She's my match."

Rolling us both over, Amy moaned as I pushed deep inside her while kissing her down her neck. Her legs curled up and her fingers dug into my shoulders, moving down to my lower back. "Mmm, Russell..."

I let one hand slide down the canyon of her breast, placing it over her heart. I felt her cardiac muscle beat fast beneath it, increasing as her impending ōrgasm neared. My mouth found her mouth and I kissed her deeply, savoring the feel of her warm soft lips against mine.

I then thrust deep inside her and she broke apart from my lips, letting out a garbled breath. She bit her lip and strained her head back into the pillows, her eyes closed, cheeks flushed. "Russell..."

I cupped her face and kissed her mouth again as my hips sped up. Her nails dug firmly into my back and her breath pitched. Then she exploded.

Crying out and screaming my name, I joined her shortly after, grunting as I spilled into the condom. By the end we were both panting, both just lying there.

After a moment, I rolled off her, removed the condom and disposed of it in her bin. When I laid back down in her bed, Amy curled up to me, placing her head on my chest. "My sister called today. She's getting divorced."

"Sorry to hear."

"No you're not."

"No I'm not."

I faintly saw her smile as she traced a random pattern over my chest and stomach with her fingertip. It tickled but felt nice. "Have you ever thought about ever marrying again?"

"No, but that would surely make your sister's life a living hell if we did that."

"Hell yeah it would," Amy snorted, fighting a smile, probably from the thought of her sister's face if she told her she was getting married while she was getting divorced. "But seriously. Have you?"

"My first marriage was a stupid mistake, Amy, I shan't attempt a second try. That would be like volunteering to step onto a grenade; It's bound to implode."

"Alright, what about kids, then? You never wanted those?"

"Are we having the talk?" I asked, giving her a deadpan look even though she couldn't see it. Hopefully she could hear the tone in my voice. "Are you asking me where this is going? Because I told you right from the start that I--"

"That you don't do love. I know," She cut me off. A smiled slipped onto her face. "And yet here we are. I didn't expect my battery supplier-slash-plaything to fall for me, yet you did. And as you should know by now, I like more than just your dick."

"What a compliment coming from a nymphomaniac."

"I know, right? Therefore, let's just give up our pride and call a spade a spade," She said, now turning over and folding her hands over my chest, leaning her chin on them. Our eyes met. "You love me, I love you. The sex is ah-maz-ing and we both clearly enjoy each other's company. You're smart as hell, I'm sexy as fuck..."

"Are you asking me to put a ring on it?"

"I'm asking you if you want to implode with me."

I looked at her for a long moment. Something - some devious part of me was yanking at my good sense, telling me I should just go for it again. Give it another shot. But my good sense - the part that was left untouched - told me I should let her down as easy as I could because it made no sense for me to marry someone again. Logically speaking and statistically speaking, we were likely to get divorced within the first year of our marriage since we were too different. In a lot of ways, she was perfect for me, but would she still be perfect with me?

Love was a fickle thing. I think the truth as to why I got divorced the first time wasn't because I got too consumed in my job. I deliberately pulled away because love was too unpredictable for me. Normally I liked dealing with stuff that was unpredictable - most things were predictable in my life, deducible, so I lacked the excitement. But I quickly learned that love was too fickle to be tampered with and I therefore decided to leave the force alone.

In other words; I was scared.

I couldn't figure it out, there was no legit mathematical equation to love. It was a mystery I couldn't solve. The chemistry of it all? Yes. But the actual logic of it? Nuh-uh. No logic.

"I can practically hear the cogwheels in your head turning," Amy chuckled, placing a velvet kiss on my chest. Her lips lingered a little, tickled my skin. She then exhaled, blowing out a warm breath through her mouth that warmed me. "I understand if you don't want to, Russ. It was just a suggestion. I just want you to know I have no expectations. I don't want a big suburban house with a white picket fence, nor do I want a heaping bunch of little rascals to run around us and give us gray hairs. This right here is enough," She smiled, her eyes fluttering up to me. "You can take it or leave it."

"Why is marriage so important to you then if you just want to keep things the way they are?"

"Because I want stability. I want to settle down but I want to do it my own way. There are more ways to be married than just one," She smiled, leaning her cheek against my chest, looking distantly at her bathroom door. "You only tried one way and that clearly didn't work out for you. Why not try another way? With me?"

I closed my eyes and sighed. I had to be seriously delusional if I thought this was going to work out. All the logic inside me was screaming; 'it doesn't make sense, it's not logical, it's not rational!' And how true it was.

But then again, neither of those things applied when it came to love. Love was the only enigma I probably never would be able to solve.

- And that to me was my greatest mystery. Why not marry it, then?

"Let's make your sister's life hell."

EPILOGUE

"**R**uuuuss!"

"For the love of God, now what?"

"Where's my shoes?"

"Did you check your feet?" I bit into my toast with a crunch and stood up from the bar stool, walking to the fridge to get the milk.

"Even if I could see them, I'd say I'm pretty sure they're not there. Russ, will you please just come help me look for them, I'm late for my appointment."

Growling, I slammed the fridge shut and chewed on my loaf of toasted bread as I walked into our bedroom. Amy stood bent over by a chair, searching through a pile of dirty clothes lying on said chair. "You just had to fucking forget your pill."

I ducked under the bed and wrestled with some dust and old clothes before I managed to fish out a pair of white sneakers. "Are these the ones you were looking for?"

Amy turned around, supporting her back from the weight of her belly. "Yes. How did they get under the bed?"

"You kicked them under there when you suddenly decided to pull me from my case and have sex with me on the floor."

"Curtesy of pregnancy hormones," Amy grabbed the shoes from my hand as I handed them to her. "How's the case coming along by the way?"

"Same way you're growing our child. Excruciatingly slow."

She smirked as she popped her feet into the sneakers with some maneuvering before stepping up to me and looping her arms around my neck. "Getting impatient, are you?"

"You know how I hate waiting, it makes me restless. I need something to do."

"Oh, I know and I promise you, you can do the first diaper change. The second one too, if you behave."

"You think you're so funny," I leaned down to her lips and she chuckled as I pressed my own against hers, showering her with my love. I couldn't even find the cynicism to care about that corny statement.

"Don't make me horny now," She smirked against my lips, grabbing the toast from my hand. She took a large bite and then chewed. "I'm so late for my appointment."

"That was my breakfast."

"Go make more, I'm making a baby here."

"And who's fault is that?"

"Yours. You need to work on your pull-out game, boo-boo."

"You forgot your pill."

"This again?" She sighed, finishing my toast. "Fine. Why don't you hang onto that and then I go see the doctor in the meantime. Weren't you working on some big important case, anyway?"

"I was, until someone misplaced their shoes."

"You misplaced your sperm, let's call it even."

"Oh for Christ sake." I ran a hand through my hair and walked back into the kitchen to make myself some new toast. "The quicker you have this baby, the better. You'll be less moody then."

"I better get to the doctor's appointment then," Amy replied, grabbing her back. "See you soon."

"Wait." I walked up to her, holding something important in my hand. "Don't forget your batteries."

I handed her the batteries and she smiled a little. She then pulled out her baby-pager and changed the old batteries with the new ones. "When you said you'd get me a different vibrator, this wasn't exactly what I had in mind."

"Well, you weren't exactly what I had in mind either, yet here we are. Now go, I have to call the DA's office. Some idiot there thinks he got the whole case figured out."

"And let me guess," Amy smirked, her hand on the doorknob to our place. "He hasn't talked to you before?"

"It's going to be the best day of his life."

"I'll send the poor guy a prayer as the gynecologist sticks the vaginal scanner up into my vagina. Tootles."

She left and I returned to my work. Nine goddamn months of this pregnant hysteria. Getting work done was nearly impossible.

I had only just dialed the DA's office when my phone rang. It was Amy. What did I just say? "Don't tell me; You lost your shoes again." I drawled into the phone.

"Russ! Water! Broke!" She panted in the other end, huffing out breaths. "Contraction! Car! Hospital! Now! Phone! Doctor!"

"Does contractions mean you can't form more than one-word-sentences?"

"RUSS!"

"Alright, I'm coming!" I yelled. "Sit tight, I'll be right down."

I ended the call and then clutched on to the back of couch I had somehow backed up against. I took a deep breath, closing my eyes. A smile slid onto my face.

I was going to be a father now.